The Other Side of the Hill

Also by Judy Gill
in Large Print:

Catherine's Image
A Harvest of Jewels

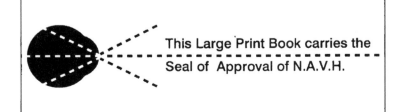

This Large Print Book carries the
Seal of Approval of N.A.V.H.

The Other Side of the Hill

Judy Gill

Thorndike Press • Waterville, Maine

Published in 2005 by arrangement with Judy Gill.

Thorndike Press® Large Print Candlelight.

The tree indicium is a trademark of Thorndike Press.

The text of this Large Print edition is unabridged.
Other aspects of the book may vary from the original edition.

Set in 16 pt. Plantin by Al Chase.

Printed in the United States on permanent paper.

Library of Congress Cataloging-in-Publication Data

Gill, Judy (Judy Griffith)
    The other side of the hill / Judy Gill.
        p. cm.
      ISBN 0-7862-7208-2 (lg. print : hc : alk. paper)
      1. Triangles (Interpersonal relations) — Fiction.
    2. British Columbia — Fiction.   3. Missing persons —
    Fiction.   4. Large type books.   I. Title.
    PR9199.3.G5298O84 2005
    813'.54—dc22   2004061731

The Other Side of the Hill

As the Founder/CEO of NAVH, the only national health agency solely devoted to those who, although not totally blind, have an eye disease which could lead to serious visual impairment, I am pleased to recognize Thorndike Press* as one of the leading publishers in the large print field.

Founded in 1954 in San Francisco to prepare large print textbooks for partially seeing children, NAVH became the pioneer and standard setting agency in the preparation of large type.

Today, those publishers who meet our standards carry the prestigious "Seal of Approval" indicating high quality large print. We are delighted that Thorndike Press is one of the publishers whose titles meet these standards. We are also pleased to recognize the significant contribution Thorndike Press is making in this important and growing field.

Lorraine H. Marchi, L.H.D.
Founder/CEO
NAVH

* Thorndike Press encompasses the following imprints: Thorndike, Wheeler, Walker and Large Print Press.

ONE

The morning sun poked fingers of light into the small, natural clearing in the forest. A bird trilled a few sharp notes, then was still, while a squirrel chittered angrily before dashing high into a fir tree. A katydid called from over the hill.

Into the clearing stepped a tall, broad shouldered man carrying in one hand a double-bitted axe while from the other swung a wicked looking machete. He stepped over a tree which had until recently been standing in the edge of the glade but was now lying prone on the mossy earth. He began to denude it swiftly of branches and bark. When the tree had become nothing more than another log, it was towed with some difficulty to a spot nearby where lay other logs.

As he worked, the muscles in the man's back and shoulders rippled, his dark hair fell with great persistence over his thick brows and into his slate-grey eyes. His big hands paused now and then in their work to brush the hair back, and one time, engaged in the act of clearing his vision, he gazed with a saddened expression upon a leafy dogwood tree and sighed heavily.

He swung his axe into a newly made stump, hung the machete by its thong from a limb and limped to the shade of the tree. His long body stretched out in the moss-filled hollow beneath the dogwood and cradling his head on his bent arms, he whispered into the moss, "Sweet lady . . . sweet lady, are you there?"

There was no answer but tender memories filled his mind; the scent of the forest, the moss, and the new warmth of the April sun brought her presence to him and as the breeze sighed through the branches, it was almost as though she were there, whispering, "Darling . . . my darling . . ."

Comforted, he slept.

The boy pelted headlong across the clearing, his footsteps muffled by the carpet of needles until he tripped over a branch protruding from the trunk of a newly fallen tree. His blue shirt caught on a sharp knot and he jerked free, sobbing gratingly between clenched teeth. His eyes were stormy and although he cried, not a tear showed. He caught sight of the axe embedded in the stump and with a strength born of anger, he grasped it and jerked it free. He hefted the axe which was nearly as long as he was tall and swung it wildly again and again, hacking small chips out of a log. As the child chopped, words came spasmodically from his contorted mouth, in time with each swing.

"I . . . HATE . . . him! I . . . HATE . . . him! I . . . HATE . . . him! There goes an . . . ARM! That was his . . . LEG! Here goes his . . . HEAD!"

The man awoke in an instant, sat up and looked in the direction from which came the sound of someone chopping erratically . . . with his axe! He saw a small, tow-headed lad swinging wildly, only one cut in three coming close to the previous marks. He rose quietly, not wanting to startle a child handling such a dangerous tool and moved toward the little boy.

As he approached, he heard the words the child was mouthing. That depth of fury, the blind, mindless anger in one so young shocked the man as did the passion of hatred which coloured the tones. This was no small boy annoyed with father or friend; this was a human soul with a deep and terrible problem!

He caught the axe handle on an upswing and held it. The boy stood stock still for a moment then let go of the axe to back away in a scurrying, scuttling manner which showed the man the child fully expected to be smacked, hard! He was poised for flight and his eyes were full of an abject terror.

The stranger's teeth gleamed white against his brown skin as he smiled at the child. "That was pretty good chopping for a young 'un," was his only comment.

As though the words had released a spring, the child shot away into the under-brush. Shrugging, the man picked up his machete from the branch upon which it hung and began stripping limbs from a fallen tree, whistling between his teeth as he worked. A flash of blue from the boy's shirt appearing at odd intervals told him he was not alone.

The squirrel, curious now, returned to watch with bright eyes the actions of the in-truder to his glade, and the man, spotting him, spoke quite loudly.

"Hello, squirrel. Did you come to help me pile up these branches? You did? Well squirrel, that's mighty nice of you, but I'm afraid you're too small. What I'd like to have to help me build this log cabin is a boy with strong arms. Sure do wish there was one around!"

The splotch of blue behind a huckleberry bush stayed quite, quite still, and the man bent, holding his back and groaning loudly as he gathered up an arm-load of branches. "Oh, that's hard on my back! Maybe I'd better leave it for another day." He dropped his load upon the pile he had already begun and ambled off, his axe across his left shoulder, the machete swinging from his right hand.

The next morning he returned and smiled to himself when he saw that every scrap of rubbish from the previous day's work had been cleared. For some time he worked and the chips flew in wide arcs, scenting the air with the perfume of newly cut wood. As each tree began to sway, the man would leap back, call, "Timberrrr!" loudly, as with a rushing of air through the flailing limbs and an earth-jarring thud, the tree fell. As each tree met the ground, a flash of red shirt would jump with what might have been excitement.

Picking up a small canvas bag, the man walked to his favourite resting place and with his back to the clearing, pulled a fat sandwich from its wrappings and began munching. "Hi there, squirrel," he said conversationally to his nearest companion. "Was it you cleared up for me yesterday? If so, then I guess the cabin will belong to both of us. After all, if two work together on something, it has to be theirs, not just the one who began it."

A stealthy rustling behind him told the man that work was underway once more, and he lay back, pretending to sleep until a distant voice raised the hair on the nape of his neck, calling, "Phillip! Phiii-llip!"

Shortly after another sunrise the glade rang again with the sound of the biting axe blade, chips flew as the child was drawn closer, closer, watchfully waiting, listening for the magic call of the word, "Timberrr!"

When he went to rest the stranger to the glade sat once more with his back to the clearing and when the whispers of sounds began, he waited for a moment or two then turned slowly. As if sensing he was under surveillance, the child froze, bent by the weight of the aromatic bundle of greenery he carried. He raised apprehensive eyes to the man then dumped his load on the pile.

"Cake?" asked the man quietly, extending a plastic wrapped object to the child.

Phillip walked closer, eyeing the cake with the normal greed of a small boy and reached for it tentatively, as if a show of eagerness might cause the offer to be rescinded.

His finely-cut jaw worked industriously for a few moments then, with a spray of crumbs, he said, "It's good," and smiled.

The stranger nodded, picked up his machete and began peeling a log. Phillip stepped closer. "What's that thing?" he asked, after watching for a long time.

"A machete," was the quiet reply. "It's supposed to be for cutting through jungles, but it peels logs pretty well, too."

There was another long pause then, "Why you want them logs peeled?"

"For the log cabin we're going to build."

"Where?"

"Right here . . . in the clearing."

"Why?"

"To live in."

"Why don't you hire a contractor? Grant gets one whenever he wants something built."

"I like to do it for myself."

"Why don't you use a chain saw to cut down the trees?"

The man bent deliberately and gathered up an armload of branches and took them to the scrap pile before he was ready to reply, and then he had to wait until Phillip had returned from doing the same. "I don't like the smell of power saws in the woods. I don't like the noise they make and I think the trees feel better about being cut down if you don't ruin their home with noisy, smelly saws. When you're cutting down a lot of

13

trees you have to use machinery, but here for our little clearing, this way's best."

The boy was not yet ready to admit this stranger was right. "Grant's contractors could have this clearing finished in one day with two power saws and one bull-dozer!"

The man nodded. "Maybe. But this is my clearing and I like doing it this way."

"Where do you live?"

He pointed to a path in the trees. "In a camper over that way. Until the cabin's finished."

"I mean where do you really live? Where's your house?"

"The camper's my home until the cabin's ready." He walked off with more branches. Phillip struggled to keep up.

"How come you limp?"

"I hurt my leg a long time ago."

"Grant fell off his horse and hurt his leg. He doesn't limp, I laughed and he was going to hit me with his crop but my mom made him stop. She told him I didn't know he was hurt and he did look funny going into the hedge."

"He must have," with a smile. Then, "Who's Grant?"

The child's answer, if it was that, was oblique. "What's a prep school? How come they dip-licine kids there?"

"I think you mean 'discipline', Phillip. It just means teaching you what's right, what's wrong and showing you how to grow up to be a good man. A prep school's like any other school. Are you going to go to one?"

"Grant said he's going to send me to one when he marries my mom. How'd you know my name?"

"Heard someone, your mom, maybe, calling you." He walked to his resting place sat down and asked the boy who had followed him like a shadow, "What's the rest of your name?"

"Phillip David Jefferson. What's yours?"

The man's hand paused in the act of removing the top from his Thermos. For a long moment he remained frozen and the child said, "What's the matter, Mister? Your face looks all funny!"

He made a great effort, poured liquid into the cap and passed it to Phillip. "Lemonade?"

Phillip gulped greedily, then passing the cap back, repeated, "What's yours?"

"Jeff," replied the man, taking an apple out of the bag. He sunk strong teeth into it and handed it to the boy. "How old are you, Phillip?"

"Seven," then thinking it might be wise to add the truth, "next month."

"What's your . . ." began Jeff, but he was interrupted by the distant call, "Phiiillip!" and his young companion leapt to his feet, calling over his shoulder, "See you, Jeff!"

Can it be? Could it be? But if it is . . . Why? In God's name, why? He hustled himself out of the clearing and his camper truck was started with a grinding of gears, a crunching of gravel and it sped away toward the nearest town.

Phillip came out of the forest at a gallop, racing down the path across the open grassy meadow and jumped the little brook on the other side of which waited his mother. She had her hands on her hips, a half-smile played around her soft mouth and her deep brown eyes with amber light in them twinkled down at him. Phillip grinned impishly at her and felt her warmth cover him. Everything about his mom was warm; the way she smiled, the way her eyes looked and most of all her hair, like the deepest coals in the fire just before it went out. A glowing, deep red.

"Hi, Mom!" he gasped, skidding to a stop in front of her then turning as always to throw a rock in the creek. "Lunch time?"

"Yes," she said, exasperatedly. "Just as it was lunch time yesterday when I had to come out here to call you. What's so good about the woods lately?"

16

"Jeff," he replied thrashing the fence with a stalk of buckwheat. "Jeff 'n' me are building a log cabin."

Eleanor smiled down at him. "That's nice, darling." For the thousandth time she wished there were more, or nearer neighbours with children Phillip's age, so her son could have some real playmates. "But don't wander too far off, will you, son?"

"I won't Mom. Just to the other side of the hill. That's where me and Jeff are building the cabin."

"Jeff and I," she corrected, absently wondering what the child psychologist would have to say about the name he had chosen for his latest imaginary friend. Would it be that in having chosen a name which could be a diminutive of his own surname he was acting out a need to have a brother? "Stay away from the Anderson house, too," she admonished. "It's private property, remember."

"Just the woods, Mom . . . and no one cares about the woods."

Later, Eleanor ran a comb through her hair and walked up the hill to the farmhouse, the house in which she had spent her childhood. She knocked at the door which had once been her own, and, in a sense, still was.

Kathy Robins opened it and smilingly invited her landlady into the big, warm kitchen. "Ellie! Come on in! Bill's just bedding down his new baby. Coffee's on. Phil sleeping?"

"Morning Glory's foaled?" Eleanor nodded in answer to Kathy's question and beamed at the news about the horse. "Hey! Don't! Let me!" she said as Kathy reached high over her head for coffee cups. "Didn't anyone tell you not to do that?"

"Old wives' tales," grinned Kathy. "Bill's mother's full of them and Bill, darn it, believes her! I hope his absorption with the foal will take his mind off his impending fatherhood for a day or two." Kathy went on about Bill and his delight in his mare's offspring. At length she subsided and looked carefully at Eleanor.

"What's the trouble, Ellie? Book not doing so well?"

"No, the book's doing just fine. It's Phil, Kathy. He's got another imaginary friend. Maybe Grant's right and I should send him away to school. It's just that he's so little!" Her voice cracked slightly and one long, slender hand rubbed her forehead as it tended to in times of stress.

"Of course he is!" said Kathy sternly.

"But he is lonely," replied Eleanor, more

in answer to herself than to her friend. "Holidays must be awful for him, like weekends and after school only lasting much longer. I wish you'd hurry up and have that lump in your lap, then he'd have that to play with."

"If said lump puts in an appearance before the middle of June it's going to have to find some other family. We simply won't be ready for it!" Kathy refilled the cups, pulled a tin of cookies closer and ate two in quick succession, managing to look contented and guilty at the same time. "But about Phillip, Ellie, it can't hurt him to have imaginary playmates. He gets along well at school with the real kids, and lots of children have pretend friends. Not just only children, either."

"No," said Eleanor wryly. "Just lonely children. As a former teacher, Kath, what do you think about sending kids away to school? Is it good for them? Especially," she added, "kids who have no one at home to play with?"

Kathy considered carefully before she answered. "Maybe, but personally, I can't think of one child from my teaching days who would have been better off away from his family. When I apply it to Phillip, think of him being sent away from here, away

19

from you, I can only see him being terribly unhappy. So maybe he is a little bit lonely; Easter holidays only last ten days and three of them are gone by. It's not going to kill him, Ellie, to have an imaginary friend for the next week. Who is it this time?"

"Someone named Jeff. They're building a log cabin together. I suppose I could put a stop to it, but it seems a shame to keep him out of the forest. He's like his father in that respect; loves the trees, the bird-song, the seclusion. I wish he'd start taking an interest in the farm. Maybe Grant's right when he says Phillip needs a man's firm hand to give him some discipline."

"But," pointed out Kathy dryly, "Grant, for all that, is the one who advocates sending him away so some school can do it. Why doesn't he try himself, starting, of course, by using some of that patience he expends on his precious horses?"

Eleanor shrugged, not willing to discuss Grant and his inability to relate to her son. "Oh," she lamented, "Where are the days of colouring books, crayons, finger-paints and Tinker Toys?"

As she walked home Eleanor waded through the long grass, dew-damp and clinging, and star-gazed, remembering the early days of her son's life, thinking back upon what it had been like, as a new mother, aged twenty, alone save for her father and infant son, never giving up the secret hope that somehow, sometime, David might come back.

Where had he gone? Was he dead as her father had thought or was he simply gone from her, unable to face the thought of being tied down by a wife and child? The David whom she had married at the age of nineteen, whom she had loved so wonderfully, and who had loved her enough to browbeat her stubborn old father into letting them marry, was not that kind of man!

He must be dead, her mind told her, while her heart denied it even after nearly eight years of silence from the jungles of Peru. "Where are you," she whispered to the stars above. "Are you anywhere in this world? Should I have you declared legally dead, or should I keep on waiting . . . hoping?"

Hoping for what? she asked herself as she had nearly every day. Hoping for the return of a man whose face has disappeared from my memory, a man, whom if he did come back, would be totally different? But people never change that much! she argued with herself. I haven't forgotten. I've never forgotten entirely. I still hear his voice in my dreams even though his face has gone from me.

But what good are dreams, Eleanor? You're twenty-seven years old; time's passing! And Grant . . . will he wait forever? Who cares? whispered a small voice deep inside her. Who cares what Grant might do?

Eleanor sighed and turned in under the rose arbour. She sank to a bench and leaned her elbows on the table. She propped her chin in her hands and let her mind wander back . . . back to the past she could remember, and the past of which her father had spoken . . . back to the day when she first met David . . .

She had wandered away from the house, needing to be alone, full of the vague sadness of a March morning after a storm. During the night the rain had come, thundering onto the roof, beating into the greyish slush left from the last . . . hopefully last and not just latest . . . snowfall. When she awoke the world was new and clean, the earth black and fruitful-looking, the sky clear and the alder trees just shaded pink with the first touch of buds on gaunt, bare limbs.

Eleanor had strolled toward the brook and stood for a time looking into the rushing brown freshet, and a longing arose in her breast, an aching need to flee, to rush and tumble headlong into life as the water at her feet was rushing away into the distance to join up with the Thompson, which in turn met the Fraser and combined with the thousands and thousands of other small creeks all over the hills and mountains of British Columbia poured into the Pacific . . . into the Pacific and away . . .

She jumped the brook, left its exciting spring-time babble behind and made for the edge of the forest, heading for her quiet place, her place of dreaming.

She entered the forest, walking silently upon the thick carpet of needles which covered the path. The moss beneath her feet was thick and wet. Mud splashed the backs of her legs, but Eleanor cared naught for that. Who was there to see her? Who was there to comment on the appearance of this girl whom no one loved as a woman longs to be loved . . . and who had no one of her own to love as a woman needs to love?

Her private place, her little glade, welcomed her with a single shaft of sunlight and Eleanor sat upon a damp log near a small dogwood tree. She put her elbows on her knees, her head in her hands and her long hair fell forward to obscure her face. She was a small and dejected wood nymph huddled there upon that log, and when the sound of an intruder entering her glade disturbed her, Eleanor's head flew up, the hair was whipped back from her face and wide, chocolate and honey eyes stared up at the tall young man who stood there.

He was thin almost to the point of emaciation. Her eyes took this in even while her heart began its wild and tumultuous thundering, feeling like the brook running away with itself into unknown territory. His slate coloured eyes stared into hers for a long, aching moment, and then he smiled. "My rad's sprung a leak," were his first words to her, and the resonance of his voice should have come from a much deeper chest than the bony one under the forestry-green work shirt.

"I . . . On the forestry road?" He nodded, and Eleanor said, "I'll get my father . . ." It hurt to speak. Her heart still thudded painfully in her breast, and those eyes, those intense, slate-grey eyes under the thick brows and dark shaggy hair refused to release her.

"Wait!" he said urgently. "Wait. What's your name?"

"Eleanor," she all but whispered, "Eleanor Barnes."

"Eleanor." He said it slowly, savouring each syllable as if it were sweet. "Eleanor," he repeated, "I'm going to marry you . . ."

TWO

Eleanor . . . I'm going to marry you! The words echoed and reechoed through the empty caverns of her heart, flooding and filling until she was no longer empty, no longer aching with the unnamed and unnameable needs of an early spring day, but spilling over with something just as unnamed, just as unnameable. She gasped, put one long slender hand to her wide and mobile mouth and fled, casting one startled glance over her shoulder at this strange young man who had come out of the forest. He was watching her go, the smile still upon his gaunt face, his eyes still glowing with a light from within.

Eleanor had run all the way home, and her father, fifty-four years old at the time of his daughter's birth, the birth which had claimed his wife, looked up, startled. His sparse hair was grey, his skin hung loosely upon his frame as though waiting to be filled out the way it had been when he was young.

"Where you been, girl?" he demanded. "What are you doing rushing around outside when there's work to be done?"

"I'm sorry, Dad. I went for a walk . . . the day was too good to waste inside. There's someone in the woods on the Anderson place. He's in the little glade just off the forestry road. His rad's sprung a leak." Eleanor gasped out the words, knowing her face was flushed. Her eyes felt bright, too, and she lowered her face before her father's keen stare.

"What is it, Ellie?" he asked sharply. "Did he scare you?"

"No!" Then, more sedately, "No, Dad. I was running because . . . because it's spring!"

A gnarled and gentle old hand stroked the deep, rich red of her hair, and George Barnes said, "Yes, Ellie-girl. Spring days are for running. Your mother was the same, girl. The same in looks, the same in actions. Then when it seemed we'd never have a child, she stopped running, stopped singing and laughing and I thought my heart would break. But one more time, girl, just one more time, she ran to me, laughing! It was the day she told me you were on the way. I picked her up and carried her back to the house, girl, and from that moment on I looked after her, cared for her as if she was made of glass . . . and what good did it do

26

me? But I have you, girl, to take her place. So like her you are Ellie, so . . ."

"Dad," interrupted Eleanor gently. "The man on the forestry road?"

"What? Oh, oh, yes. I'll take a bucket and get him some water from the creek over there."

She watched with a deep affection as her father walked away, bent yet still moving strongly for all his seventy-three years.

Having never known her mother, except through her father's stories, Eleanor had what may have been more than the usual amount of love for her dad, and he, on his part, loved his daughter beyond all else. She was his life.

When he had been left a widower with an infant daughter to raise, he had flatly refused all offers of help from the neighbours. Many times he had told her that he had raised her the same way he would have raised on orphaned calf; with good, common sense and outsized portions of love. It worked on the calves, and it had worked on her. Eleanor had grown up knowing little beyond her own immediate locality, and if a longing built in her now and then for far places and new sights, as it had this morning, she could always push it back and look around, happy with her lot.

George had insisted that Eleanor finish high school, but when she had graduated with honours, had put his foot down firmly to scotch any ideas her counsellor had put into her head about university. "No, girl, I raised you and you stay here. You have all the learning you can get out of books, all you'll ever need, that is!"

She had put up a small argument. The fusty old professors, musty libraries, parties, room-mates, dormitory life had sounded like heaven to her, and what would . . . must! come after, knowing about the world, seeing it for herself, had been brought tantalisingly close by her counsellor's words. George remained adamant, and his daughter, accustomed to obeying, stayed.

She had become a wonderful cook over the years of her teens, an excellent housekeeper. She sewed, knit, gardened. Her flowers were a riot of colour; her vegetables abundant and flavourful, and she worked long, hard hours willingly, beside her ageing father, helping him to run his dairy farm.

Throughout her high school years, and in the past year since she had been at home all day, boys and young men had come to call, but each came only once, until there were no more left to come at all and Eleanor became as much of a recluse as her father.

28

But today! And Eleanor wrapped her arms around herself, spun in a dizzy circle, and laughed aloud at the hens scattering and cackling in her path. Today she had met someone whom she knew would not be put off by her irascible old father! How can it happen like that? she wondered. And what is it, exactly, has happened?

She knew a little later when a clanking old pick-up truck came limping into the barnyard and the lanky young man climbed out. Her father got out of the passenger side and the two men stood talking for some time. Suddenly the young man put a hand to his head, swayed on his feet and old George put out a hand to steady him. Her father spoke, and Eleanor could not hear his words, but she could see concern reflected on his face. The young man answered, George spoke again, and the other shook his head, still holding the side of the truck. This time her father did not bother speaking but grasped the green-clad arm, draped it over his stooped shoulders and half-dragged, half-carried his burden into the kitchen where Eleanor stood, staring.

"What is it?" she asked, looking at her father.

"The boy needs food!" George replied. "Look at him — skinny as a rake, almost fainting from hunger. Well, don't just stand there, girl, get cooking! I'll get some brandy!" And as George stomped out, Eleanor looked at the young man slumped in the chair.

His eyes were dancing with laughter and he winked at her. "I had to see you again," he whispered. "This was the only way I could get invited to lunch. No! Don't back away. You have been chosen." As George returned, he lay back again, looking wan. Eleanor scurried to do things at the stove.

"What's your name, boy?" asked George, as he shovelled hot stew and over-warm bread into himself.

"David Jefferson, sir."

"I'm George Barnes. This is my daughter, Ellie."

"No, sir. Eleanor," David said, and again his resonant voice caressed her name. "Don't call her 'Ellie', please, Mr. Barnes."

George's beady-eyed stare raked the face of the young man as he said, "What's it to you?"

"Eleanor is going to be my wife, sir."

"Eh? What? The hell she is!"

Eleanor held her breath. "Yes, sir!" was the confident reply. "You'll see. Just wait."

"What do you do, boy?"

"I'm a forestry student. I'll be working in

the area for the next few months. You'll get used to me."

George said, "Humph!" and the meal was finished in silence.

"Where do you live?" George pushed the sugar bowl closer to his young guest.

"In town. In a rooming house. The meals are nothing like this. Thanks for the lunch, Eleanor. When I get the rad fixed, I'll be back. So long Mr. Barnes."

"Humph!" said George again.

And David had come back. He came back that very evening to take Eleanor to the movies. George said. "No. She's got to help me with the milking. Machine's broken down."

"I'll milk," said David, and did. When he was finished, he said, "Go get a dress on, Eleanor. I'll fix the machine while you change." He did that, too, and as David washed up, Eleanor could see her father eyeing him with grudging admiration.

Three weeks later Eleanor bowed to the inevitable and agreed to marry David. George, however, continued to hold out, and in spite of this David won his permission to build a small cottage in the hollow below the farmhouse, secluded by a grove of poplar trees. "Don't mind renting you the land, Dave," said the old man. "I'm not using it."

"We'll live there, George, Eleanor and I, when we're married. You can visit us any time you want . . . within reason," David had added sternly.

"You're not marrying my girl, boy!" George had said and said, and said again, right up to the day of the wedding, and on that day what he said was, "So you married her, boy! But remember this: She's my girl. I'll share her with you if I must, but just don't you ever try to take her away. Do that and I'll fight. I'll win, too!" he had added warningly.

With his arm firm around Eleanor's waist, David had replied, "She may be your girl, George, but she's my woman. Where I go, she goes, and not you or anyone else will stop her. So don't go laying down any laws!"

But someone else had stopped her, Eleanor reflected as she sat there in the rose arbour on that cool April evening nearly eight years later. Her son . . . her son and David's had stopped her, and then it was too late.

She could still bring back the wonder of that late August afternoon when David had come upon her grubbing in the roots of the scraggly little rose bushes at the foot of the arbour he had built for her. They had been married a month and already she thought she knew every nuance of his voice, every expression of his face; but today there was something different, a special tenderness, a deeper timbre in his tone and a suppressed excitement as he laughed at her labours, saying, "Never in a million years, sweet lady, will those roses cover that wood!" The slats of the arbour were raw and unplaned, stark in their newness, glaring yellow against the backdrop of leafy poplars.

Eleanor smiled up at him. "You'll see, my darling. They'll grow."

He had drawn her to her feet and kissed her then, and hand in hand they had ambled over the little brook, past the back of the farmhouse and into the dark forest to the little glade where they had met.

And that day, in that glade, with all the wildly sweet and passionate love between them, they had created life . . .

And David Phillip Jefferson had never laid eyes upon Phillip David Jefferson, for that afternoon, as they lay in each other's arms on the thick, soft moss in their forest bed, the reason for the excitement in David was given to his wife.

He had been offered a position in the forestry department of the Government of Peru, and he had snapped it up, knowing that Eleanor would want him to take it as much as he himself wanted to have it. Eleanor felt grief at the thought of having to leave her aged father, but the wonder of a life which would allow her to walk hand in hand with her husband through the forests of the world far outweighed that.

"Sweet lady," said David, there in the shade of the dogwood tree, "We'll go then. I leave tomorrow. I know I should have told you sooner, but I was so afraid if there was time for discussion, your father would try to hold us back. You'll have to stay until I can find a place for us to live, but then I'll send for you. It won't be long!" he cried, his slate grey eyes looking at her with undisguised lust, "For I can't live long without you!"

So Eleanor had waved goodbye to her love the next morning, smiling for him, saving her tears for later. He had written long screeds, for once there, he had found that he must go into the jungle for further training. He would send for her in three months when his training was completed.

Just as his letters to her were full of love, so were hers to him, and it was with joy that she wrote of her pregnancy even though it meant she was unable to travel just yet. She would be with him long before the baby was due, but if he could just be patient until the sickness was over . . .

And there was a great deal of sickness, so much in fact that her old father had no difficulty in moving Eleanor out of her little cottage and back to the farmhouse with him.

It was there in the farmhouse kitchen where she had first cooked a meal for David, that day he had faked a fainting spell so he could see her again, that she stood, as her father, with a grave face, tore Eleanor's world apart. He read her the wire which told her that David was missing with three others somewhere in the jungle. A search was underway, but little hope could be held for the safe return of the party.

At first she was inconsolable and her father grew more and more desperate as he realised at last the depth of the love his daughter had for the man who had wanted to take her from him. He tried to console her by saying that "the boy" would return, that it could take weeks to travel only a short distance in the jungle, that all she had to do was have hope.

At length, he recognised the futility, not only to her, but to himself, of his preaching hope to the heartsick girl. He gave up trying to bolster her. She must begin to forget, now, he told her. Begin to live again for herself, for her father, and for her unborn child. Her man was dead, and the sooner she quit moping and weeping for someone she could not bring back, the better it would be for all of them.

Eleanor pulled her grief inside herself, tucked it away and got on with the business of becoming a mother. But her father's words had upon her a reaction he neither expected, nor ever suspected when she heard him say what she had said all along, that David was dead. Instead of being held in a thrall of hopelessness, she felt a small spark of defiance of the fates begin to take root in her heart.

Old George began to relax, thinking his daughter had got over her grief, and maybe even begun to cease loving the memory of her husband. After all, George reasoned, they had known each other such a short time, had been married only a month. How deep could the roots of love have grown in such a short time? It was all for the best that she forget the boy.

What George did not know, however, was that the tiny seed of hope in Eleanor's heart had taken root, and was growing daily into a strong, healthy plant which, in spite of all odds, refused to die. It stayed with her, day and night, from summer into each succeeding winter and grew higher every spring when the roses on the arbour spread their tendrils longer and farther, until hope filled her soul as the soft green climbers covered the wood, now grey with age and weather.

Phillip had been born on a gentle May morning just as the sun rose. The doctor and nurse, for the sake of the old man more than the mother, who seemed not to care, had agreed to deliver the child at home, rather than in hospital. The nurse looked down at the face of the new mother as she held her son for the first time. Tears ran down the pale cheeks and the nurse had mopped them up, asking kindly if there were something Mrs. Jefferson wanted.

"I want to go home," Eleanor had whispered, and the other woman had patted her comfortingly, thinking, the poor child's still dopey. What is this, if not her home?

It took three years and a further trauma, though not an unexpected one this time, for Eleanor to go home to her little cottage with her son. The day she laid her father to rest she packed up her belongings and Phillip's and carried them alone to the little house at the bottom of the hill.

She rented the farm and house to Bill and Kathy and tried to write. Eleanor smiled, there in the dark rose arbour, as she remembered the days four years before when life had been so difficult and yet so simple.

She and Phillip might well have starved if they had had to rely on her writing for a living. It was the income from the rental of the farm, plus the fact that most of her foodstuffs were free, that had kept them going.

Rejection slips had piled up in a drawer, manuscripts littered her living room and still no one was interested in what she had to offer. They were good stories; this Eleanor knew, yet she was unable to find the one editor, the one firm of publishers out of the thousands available, who could see value in her work. Then came Grant Appleton.

Grant . . . short, stocky and quick moving, a bulldog, a go-getter of a man, bought a seedy, rundown old road house and turned it, with much hard work, into a prosperous motel. He had cabins built, a massive swimming pool, riding stables, and an excellent dining room. This last was where Eleanor came in.

Grant appeared at the farm one day when the tenant farmers were out. He came, instead, to the cottage. He was wanting a steady source of fresh fruits and vegetables in season, plus top-quality dairy products. Could they provide them? They could, and did, and Grant, intrigued by this lovely, sad-eyed woman who called herself Mrs. Jefferson, yet had no husband in evidence, returned again and again.

Eleanor welcomed his friendly visits in the evenings while her small son slept. She was, she had to admit, lonely. Her tenants, newly married, wouldn't want her presence very often, and although they repeatedly offered her and Phillip meals and hospitality, Eleanor, more often than not, refused. She remembered the time she had had with David, remembered how short it had been, and how she had resented, in retrospect, having had to share him.

Grant, seeing the litter on her desk, had picked up a few of the typewritten sheets and begun reading. "I like this," he said after a few pages. "Who have you sent it to, if anyone?" Eleanor explained her inability to interest anyone in her ideas, and Grant said, "Let me send it to my brother. He's an editor with a firm which publishes books for schools . . . not texts, but supplementary readers."

And at last Eleanor had had her break. Frank Appleton, on Grant's recommendation, had read her work, and Eleanor Bear, as she called herself, was launched with her first adaptation of B. C. Indian legends, made suitable for, and interesting to, school children.

The main difficulty in her friendship with Grant, right from the outset, had been his inability to get along with Phillip. He called Phillip spoiled, which he was not; a crybaby, which he was not; claiming frequently that all the child needed was some firm discipline to make him into a man.

"What three and a half year old child needs to act like a man?" was the indignant question of the mother.

When Phillip started kindergarten at the age of five, Eleanor was left on her own all morning. Grant, who by then had the motel operating in such a manner that he could leave it in the capable hands of his manager, started taking Eleanor for long, meandering drives, or just sitting in her house with her, and began to try to make love to her.

"Ellie," he said, "you've got to give up on the guy! If he'd been going to come back, he'd have done it years ago. It's no good hanging onto the past. I'm here! And I want you!"

She had accepted his kisses; they made her feel warm and comforted. She had accepted his gifts; it was easier to do so than to argue. But she would not accept the ring he offered her for Christmas.

"I can't wear your ring, Grant. I'm a married woman," she pointed out gently.

"Then get unmarried!" he'd cried. "For heaven's sake, Ellie, neither of us is getting any younger! And not only that, the kid needs a father!"

"I can't get unmarried," she replied, taking no notice of the rest of his speech. "If you're talking of divorce, I have no grounds."

"Desertion?"

"Not enough for me. I don't know that I've been deserted!"

"I want to marry you, Ellie!" he stormed, shaking her by the shoulders in his rage and frustration. "Let the past go!"

"I can't marry you! I have a husband!"

"He's dead!"

"Maybe . . . but my heart tells me he's not; the law says I must wait seven years to be sure."

Grant ignored that part about the law and pounced again, having heard the small element of doubt in her tone. "Ah, Ellie! Let your heart tell you to belong to me. Let me look after you! No one need know about your past. We'll go away, live somewhere else! I love you and if you can't let me be your husband, then . . ."

"Grant! Grant . . . I couldn't live . . . that way! Even if I loved you and I don't think I do, not enough, anyway, I couldn't do that!

Oh, I know first love is hard to compete with but there should be more to what I feel for you. Maybe when the seven years are up, if there's been no word, I'll think about it again. But give me that time, Grant. Please! I need it. If you don't want to, then we won't see each other anymore. It's not fair to you."

He had quit pushing her for an answer then, and the last year had been peaceful, companionable and full of his kindness to her. They dined at his motel, made trips to the city now and then, danced, skied, rode. But for all that, Grant could not put himself across to Phillip.

When, in December, just four months ago, the seven years since David's disappearance had been completed, Grant had started again. And not only did he push Eleanor for a decision, he leaned heavily on Phillip, too, trying to break him in, he said, for the coming marriage . . . a marriage to which Eleanor had not yet agreed.

Poor little Phillip, thought Eleanor, swatting a mosquito. He can't help being afraid of horses, and Grant is so darned impatient with him! The other day, when he picked him up and flung him into the saddle, Phil was so terrified! How I hated Grant in that moment, even though I knew he thought he was helping Phillip get over his fear, as well as teaching him a lesson.

Eleanor rose and walked into the house. She tried to close the screen door quietly, but as always, it squeaked. She tiptoed into the child's room and stood looking down at him in the dim light from the hallway.

His fair hair, inherited from his grandfather, was damp with perspiration, sticking up all over his head. His left foot and leg were outside the covers and she automatically tucked them in again, knowing that they would be out once more, in ten minutes. Phillip frowned and muttered something which sounded like, "I hate him!" He was talking in his sleep, his mother knew, and she thought he must be dreaming about fighting with one of his school-mates. She smiled gently at the frowning little face crushed against the pillow.

Phillip had finally stopped having nightmares, although he still talked out in his sleep occasionally. He'd done it last night, and the night before, too. The scare he'd had on the horse could possibly be blamed for that. Eleanor closed the door gently behind herself as she left her son to his dreams.

She undressed, showered and then stood in front of the double bed she still used; they had bought it together, and she could not bring herself to give it up. She twisted the wedding band she still wore and examined her body closely in the full-length mirror. No drooping or sagging, yet, she reflected, but there were those little lines around her eyes, and the grooves of sadness between her nose and mouth, visible, especially when she was tired, as now.

I'm twenty-seven, she told herself, nearly twenty-eight, and though it only shows a bit, Grant is right. Time is passing . . . neither of us is getting younger. But how can I marry him, knowing the way it is with him and Phillip?

The sight of Grant doing what could only be termed "showing off", three days before had imprinted itself on her memory. He had come galloping up full-tilt toward the hedge which surrounded the farmhouse, on his new horse, Glider. He thundered across the field, intending, they could all see, to hurdle the shrubbery. At the last minute the horse had balked and Grant had sailed up and over its neck to land in the hedge unharmed. Phillip had laughed. Eleanor had to admit that Grant did look funny with one leg stuck in the bushes, his head hanging down, and how were they to know he had bruised his knee?

Grant had got to his feet, his face was red with white patches and his eyes looked utterly mad, as for a moment he had threatened the little boy with his riding crop. She had stopped him in time, of course, and he had said immediately that he wouldn't really have whipped Phillip.

"But," Grant had added, "He does have to learn not to laugh at others and he has to get over his fear! That's why I brought Glider over." Then, before Eleanor could prevent it, Grant had tossed the little boy up into the saddle, jeering, "If you're so damned smart, let's see what you can do!"

Phillip, of course, had screeched and clung to Glider's mane, howling like a banshee. The horse had bolted, and if it hadn't been for Bill, who was nearby on his own horse, might have run away with Phillip and hurt him badly. Bill had caught the big black's reins and taken the child from the saddle. Phillip had run off into the woods, not to return to the house until late in the day.

He had obviously hidden until he knew Grant would be gone, and while he hid there in the peace of the forest, had dreamed up this latest playmate for himself.

Oh, well, yawned Eleanor tiredly, I'll leave him to it for now. She slipped between the sheets thinking, he'll be back in school before long, and it's a while until summer holidays. By then he'll have forgotten . . .

THREE

The yellow school bus trundled down the narrow road and shuddered to a stop before the doors hissed open to release Phillip at the end of the driveway. Eleanor, leaning on the fence, raised her hand to wave to her son who came galloping up toward her, lunch box banging against his knee, plastic bag full of what she knew would be weird and wonderful drawings to be hung all over the kitchen walls.

"Hi, Mom!" Phillip panted. Never could that child walk, and arrive anywhere in a condition less than out of breath! his mother thought as she bent to kiss him.

"Good day, son?" she asked as hand in hand they walked up the rutted lane to their cottage.

"Yup," was the answer. "I punched Jamie Peters on the school bus."

"What for?" Eleanor glared at her son as she pushed the door open.

" 'Cause he pulled Lorna's hair."

"Oh . . . I see. Well, why not let Lorna fight her own battles?"

"Oh, I'd have punched him anyway. I don't like him!" Phillip kicked off his school shoes, looked behind the kitchen door for his sneakers, gave his mother an accusatorial look which she answered by saying, "Ever think of looking in your closet? Some things do get put away, you know!"

"Can I go barefoot, Mom?"

Eleanor made a production of walking to the window and gazing out and up. "Snow's still on the mountain," she said. Phillip, who knew quite well there was still snow on the mountain, and therefore knew as well that he could not go barefoot, was ever hopeful that just once his mother might forget to check. He sighed.

Phillip dashed to his room, from which emitted terrible noises for a few moments, then an ominous silence.

"Hang up your pants!" Eleanor called, and was rewarded by hearing the closet door squeak open then shut with a crash. "And come get your shoes!"

Phillip pelted back to the kitchen, skidded to a stop complete with squealing-brakes-sound-effects, grinned his most engagingly, and said, "Did you remember to make doughnuts today? Sticky doughnuts?"

"One sticky doughnut coming right up,

sir," Eleanor replied, opening the can and handing him one. She licked her fingers, then her lips and dipped into the can again, this time retaining the doughnut and biting into it. "I shouldn't," she said. "I'm going to get fat!"

Phillip hooted. "Aw Mom! You won't get fat!" Then, still holding his own doughnut, he said, "Uh . . . could I have another one, please? For Jeff?"

"Oh?" Eleanor pursed her mouth, cocked her head to one side and said, "You really think 'Jeff' needs a doughnut?"

"Uh hum," nodded her serious-faced little son. "He doesn't have a mom to look after him and he lives in a camper. He c'n make cakes 'n' things in his little oven, but he couldn't make these." Phillip waved his doughnut and sticky crumbs of icing fell all over the floor. "He doesn't have a deep-fryer."

More to save her floor than anything else, Eleanor gave Phillip the extra treat he had requested and pushed him out the door. "O.K., O.K.," she laughed. "After a story as full of details as that, I guess you deserve one for 'Jeff'."

As Phillip warmed up his jets for takeoff, his mother called loudly above the racket. "And don't be late! We're going out for dinner with Grant!"

The whining jets suffered an abrupt flameout and Phillip protested. "Aw, Mom, can't I have dinner with Kathy and Bill? Or . . ." hopefully, ". . . Jeff?"

Eleanor ruffled his hair. "Not tonight, love. Grant's going to ask the cook to make a big juicy hamburger for you, with cheese, bacon, tomatoes and lots of sauce. Sound good?"

"Chips, too?"

"Chips, too."

Waving the two sticky doughnuts from his wingtips, Starfighter Phillip screamed away, kicking in his afterburners as he soared out over the rapidly diminishing terrain three thousand miles below him. Boy, he thought, nobody's ever taken one of these birds this high before!

In a flash he had found the section of forest he wanted and the Starfighter became a helicopter which was landed with great expertise and all the correct sound-effects, in the clearing.

The glade was empty and the pilot stood near his machine looking for the enemy. The sound of a truck in low gear alerted him and he huddled behind a bush, lurking . . . waiting. In the month since school had been back in after Easter, much had been done in the clearing, and as always, Jeff had left quite a bit for Phillip to do this afternoon.

There were littered patches beside naked logs, underbrush still to be uprooted or cut back, and the helicopter pilot forgot his mission as Jeff limped into the clearing. "Hi, Jeff! Want a doughnut?"

A smile lit the face of the man. "Surely would like a doughnut, sport," he said. Phillip produced the pair of sticky buns and leaning against a stump, the two munched in companionable silence until the last crumbling bit of icing had been licked from each finger. Jeff said, brushing icing off his short, curly beard, "That was great! Who made 'em?"

"My mom. She's a good cooker. I'll bring you another one after school tomorrow."

"That'd be nice, Phil, but if you keep bringing me goodies like that, I'm going to end up looking like a big old tub!" He picked up his axe and began limbing a tree which lay on the ground.

"That's what my mom said, that she'd get fat if she ate her doughnut."

Jeff leaned on the handle of his axe and looked quizzically at the boy. "Your mom isn't fat is she?"

"Naw! She's skinny. Grant says she doesn't eat enough. We're going out to dinner at the motel tonight with Grant and I'm getting a gooey hamburger with cheese and bacon and tomatoes and chips too!"

"Chips too? Can you eat all that?"

"Sure! I've got a hollow leg."

"It sounds like a good dinner. I'd like to have that, too. Where is this motel you and your mom and Grant are going to?"

"Oh, Grant doesn't have to go to it! He lives there. It's his. Appleton's Motor Hotel. You know."

"Ah . . . yes," said Jeff slowly. "I know. I've driven by it. Pool, air-conditioning, gourmet dining . . . that the one?"

"Yup. Hey, Jeff, why'n't you come too? We always have a table right by the windows and there's four chairs and only three of us to sit there."

"Well, sport, that's a nice thought, but it's not such a good idea. You see, if your mom and Grant are going to get married, then they probably like to keep things like dinners sort of a family-type evening. He'll be your stepfather when they marry, you know."

"Yeah . . . I know." Phillip had no idea how revealing his answer was to his friend.

"When do they plan to get married, son?" asked Jeff with an odd note in his voice.

"Grant says the minute my mom stops

acting like a love-lorna girl and tells the judge to say my father's dead. What's a love-lorna girl?"

Jeff's face relaxed from its tight lines and he grinned at the child. "I think you mean 'love-lorn', Phillip. It means she's in love with someone."

"Oh, yeah. Grant says she only thinks she is because she can't love a ghost for the rest of her life. My mom says she doesn't know who she's in love with unless it's me and her typewriter. I asked her about it after I heard her and Grant fighting one night when they thought I was asleep." He cocked his head on one side and Jeff felt his heart tumble painfully at the so familiar mannerism; so familiar, and last seen so long before . . .

Phillip's voice broke into his thoughts. "Hey, Jeff . . ." He frowned, as if unsure of the rightness of asking this question.

"What is it, Phil?"

"Well . . . When Grant was yelling at my mom, he said it was crimmle to let a double bed go to waste like that. I know a crimmle is someone who has to go to jail, and my mom laughed when I asked her and said she wasn't being crimmle at all and not to worry about what Grant says. She's not going to go to jail, is she?"

"No, son! She is most definitely not going

to go to jail!" replied Jeff emphatically. "Tell me, Phillip, what does your mom look like?"

Phillip thought hard for a moment. "She's kinda pretty. Not like Miss Walker, but she's O.K."

"Is her hair black, brown, grey?"

"No-o-o. It's kinda like . . . like . . . like a rootbeer popsicle! And so are her eyes."

Jeff threw back his head and roared with laughter. "A rootbeer popsicle! Oh, Phil, that's wonderful! Who," he asked, sobering somewhat, "is Miss Walker?"

"She's my teacher. She has real pretty brown hair and it's always blowing in the wind when we're outside playing. She c'n run faster than me and she has blue eyes. She's real pretty!"

"She sounds it . . . so you think your teacher's prettier than your mom, do you?"

"Well . . . maybe not much, but a little bit. She's not quite as nice, though. I love my mom best. Better even than Lorna."

"Another girl in your life? Who's Lorna?" There was absolutely no work being done on the cabin today!

"She's my girl-friend. I think I love her. That's why I thought Grant was saying love-lorna. I figured maybe my mom loved Lorna, too."

Jeff laughed deep in his throat and rubbed his hand over the blond head by his knee. "Well, sport, there's lots of time for you to think about loving Lorna. Right now we have a cabin to build. I don't want to be living in the camper come winter, so let's get on with this before the snow flies. What kind of fireplace should we make? Stone, or brick?"

"Oh, stone," replied Phillip, earnestly and without hesitation. "Stone's the nicest. The one in Grant's dining room is made out of orange metal and it doesn't even look like a fireplace. The one in our house is made out of big, grey stones. My father built it, Mom says. She said he could build anything. I wish we had a picture of him, but we don't."

"What do you know about your father, Phil?"

"He is tall and skinny and has eyes like mine."

"That's all?"

"Well, my mom says he's a hard act to follow . . . she didn't say that to me, though . . . to Grant . . . and he likes trees and he went away to the jungles."

Jeff raised his head, turned his face away from Phillip and swallowed hard. "Listen," he said. "Is that your mom calling you?"

And sure enough, faint and far away, came the high, clear call.

"That's her! See you tomorrow, Jeff!"

"No . . . see you tonight, Phillip. I'm going to the motel for dinner, too. But . . ." He hesitated for a moment, eyeing the boy, and Phillip interrupted.

"Are you?" His eyes were alight. "But listen, Jeff . . ." Phillip's ears turned pink. "You won't say anything to . . . anybody about Lorna; will you?"

"Of course not. Wouldn't you like your mom to know you had another girl besides her?"

"Oh, Mom wouldn't mind! But Grant . . . he'd make fun of me."

"I won't say a word, sport. But tell you what; just in case I forget, and mention it, we'll pretend we're strangers not even say 'Hi' to each other. It'll be our secret that we're friends building a log cabin together. O.K.?"

"Sure, Jeff!" And the call came again, still faint, but with an undertone which meant business.

Phillip broke cover at the crest of the hill and ran, firing his rifle into the hordes of Indians who filled the bottom of the valley. Single-handed, he wiped out eighteen of them, dodging wildly from pine tree to pine tree. The remainder leapt upon their pintos and galloped out across the prairie, leaving behind a beautiful Indian Princess whom Phillip caught by the hand and dragged away.

"I caught you, Indian Princess! I'm going to steal you and hide you and those braves," he waved a disdainful hand at the departing Indians, "will never find you again! HaaiiEEE!"

And the Indian Princess, who had been about to lay some rawhide across a small bottom, instead cowered away from the intrepid cowboy and said, "Oh, please, please, brave cowboy, let me go! I must go back to the teepee of my father! If I don't . . . he won't let you have a gooey hamburger for dinner!"

Phillip glowered at his mother. "He's not your father, or mine, either!"

Briefly taken aback by the vehemence in her son's tone, Eleanor paused for a moment before she spoke. Then she said, "Wouldn't you like to have a father, Phil . . . to have Grant as a father?"

Phillip considered carefully for a moment as they walked on. "Would we live in the motel, swim in the pool and eat in the dining room all the time?"

"Well, you could swim in the pool all you liked, but Grant would build us a house, and I'd make all our meals in our own kitchen."

"Would Grant build the house his ownself?"

"No, of course not, really, darling," said Eleanor, towing her son along behind her. "He'd have it built for us, though, and it would be ours. We'd all three live in it, and be a real family."

"Then I'll go live in the cabin with Jeff. We're building that our ownselfs."

"Ourselves, Phillip," corrected Eleanor, dropping the subject.

The dining room was fairly crowded that evening when Eleanor entered on Grant's arm with her son bouncing along behind, peering interestedly into other peoples' plates. Grant solicitously held out Eleanor's chair, saw that Phillip sat down, and then seated himself with his back to the window, surveying his domain with a proud look. He ordered for them, and while the two adults sipped a dry sherry from Grant's private stock, Phillip fidgeted, twisting around, craning his neck, trying to see behind himself.

"What's the trouble, son?" asked Eleanor.

"I want to sit where Grant is. I can't see . . . anything."

"What's wrong with the view out the window?" asked Grant testily.

Eleanor patted his hand placatingly. "Grant, when you're not quite seven, the view in the other direction is always more interesting. Won't you trade places with him, please?"

Making no attempt to conceal his displeasure, Grant got up with ill grace and Phillip darted around the table, beaming. Instead of taking the chair he had vacated, however, Grant swung another chair around and sat opposite Eleanor. She suppressed a smile of amusement. He doesn't like to have his back to the room any more than Phillip does!

The meal arrived and while she ate, Eleanor was aware of her son's smiling secretly now and then at someone across the crowded room. She turned her head but could spot no one familiar, not even the James family who had that sweet little brown-haired daughter, Lorna; the Lorna who had taken up so much of Phillip's attention not long ago.

Eleanor, still looking out over the room, smiled absently, thinking, Lorna this, Lorna that. Lorna said, did, is, was . . . And her son said he didn't like girls much! But now it was Jeff this, Jeff that . . .

Suddenly she felt a pair of eyes catch her glance and for one heart-stopping moment it felt like the floor swooped out from under her chair. Something caught in her chest as she looked right into the eyes of a strange man whose beard obscured most of his face. The feeling in her breast was almost a physical pain and she turned with difficulty to Grant, forcing a laugh at something he'd said, something she had failed to hear.

"What's with you?" he asked, annoyed. "I asked you twice if you wanted more coffee, and all you can do is laugh at me?"

"Sorry, Grant . . . sorry. I was thinking of some . . . thing else." Now why in the world had she almost said someone? "No, no more, thanks. I have to get Phillip home to bed. School tomorrow."

"Let's bed him down here," said Grant, quietly but urgently. "We can put him in my spare room and come back and dance for a while. You spend the night, too, Ellie. We can send him off to school from here."

With a quick glance at her son who was smiling sleepily out into the dining room, oblivious to the conversation of his elders, she said quietly, "And do you have a spare room for me? The motel looks pretty packed, Grant."

Grant slowly shook his head. His eyes raked her hotly from her hair to her breasts, to her narrow waist. "Ellie," he said, reaching for her arm across the table, his warm fingers wrapping tightly around her wrist, "you know where I want you to sleep. Stay with me tonight! You know very well I had no intention of your sleeping anywhere but in my bed, so why be coy about it?" His fingers moved higher on her arm, burning as they caressed the soft skin just below her shoulder.

She moved herself out of reach. "Grant, how many times do we have to go through this? You know my answer in advance, so why ask?"

His eyes smouldered and his round face took on an ugly look. "Ah, you're probably frigid, anyway!" he hissed between his teeth.

"I guess you'll never know, will you?" asked Eleanor sharply. And she took her son by the hand and marched out, head held high.

Eleanor hustled Phillip across the parking lot, her heels ringing angrily on the concrete. As she neared her car, she saw the broad shoulders of the bearded man whose glance she had intercepted in the dining room. She noticed with detachment that he had a limp, and wondered briefly where he was from. He was climbing into a dirty, dented camper which looked as if it had been given some hard use on bad roads, although it was not old.

He paused in the act of lifting his game leg into the driver's door, and turned, his teeth showing white as he grinned in delight at Phillip's words. Eleanor wished her son did not have such a clear, piping voice, for what the man heard, what he grinned at, was: "Mom, what's frigid?"

"Not now, Phillip!" she snapped impatiently. "I'm too tired to explain, and besides, you should not listen to conversations which don't concern you!" She bundled Phillip into the back seat of the car and drove away from the motel, noticing the lights of the camper following her as she made for home. He stayed with her until she turned off the main road, then continued on toward the Exley place. Maybe he's a friend of theirs, she thought idly, turning out the headlights and shutting off the engine. It crackled and popped loudly in the still night as it cooled and Eleanor hauled her sleepy child out of the car. Her mind was still unnaturally occupied with the bearded stranger, and she couldn't for the life of her have said why. There are no campsites out that way, and if he'd been staying with Ralph and Joanne they would have been out for dinner with him. I wonder if he's freeloading on the Anderson place?

Eleanor pulled Phillip's sweater off over his head and she asked, as he appeared from inside it all tousled and bleary-eyed, "Son, are there any strangers around? Have you seen anybody in the woods who didn't belong?"

Phillip yawned and shook his head negatively.

As she tucked him into his bed, he said in his can't-keep-it-to-myself-any-longer voice, "Did you see him, Mom? Jeff? He had dinner with us at the motel!"

So that's what he'd been smiling at all evening! Not, as she'd thought, someone across the room, but at his own imaginary friend right across the table from him! That, too, explained why he had wanted to change places with Grant. He must have reasoned that if he did change, Grant would sit at the side of the table, leaving the chair opposite Phillip free for 'Jeff'. Friends, of course, must sit across from one another! "Oh, really darling?" she smiled. "What did 'Jeff' eat for dinner?"

"Didn't you see? The same as me! You looked right at him, Mom. You smiled."

"Oh, yes," said Eleanor, switching off the light. "I remember now."

Eleanor sat at her desk beside the fireplace, a blank page of paper in her typewriter, copy beside her, and her hands lay idle in her lap. Why oh why, did Grant have to start that business again? I thought he was going to give me more time to think! He's never been stupid enough to proposition me right in front of my son before, so what was the problem tonight?

It must have been the dress . . . the perfume.

She had chosen the dress with care, wanting to look nice, to please Grant . . . it was a deep green silk which did marvellous things for her complexion and figure, and she'd piled her hair high on her head, leaving little tendrils hanging in front of her ears, and one to lie seductively on the nape of her neck. It was my own fault, she decided. If I don't want to turn him on, then I should take care that I don't dress the way he likes.

But, darn it! I like dressing up! And I don't see why I should have to go around in a gunny sack just so Grant can keep his hands and his eyes to himself! To say nothing of his thoughts! But why should I feel angry that he wants me? My goodness, we're both adults. Maybe he's right . . . maybe I am frigid. But I don't think so . . . with David I was anything but.

David . . . A sweet smile of remembrance curved Eleanor's lips and softened her eyes for a long, long moment. She drew in a deep breath and let it out slowly.

Suddenly, with a start, she leapt to her feet, the horrible conviction that she was being stared at from out of the night coming over her in a wave of goose-pimples. She pulled her sheer negligée closer around herself and went to the window, wondering for an instant if Grant had followed her home. She stared out into the darkness for a moment, then, realising that if there were someone out there, she was giving them a marvellous peep-show with the light behind her, she jerked the drapes closed.

Back at her typewriter Eleanor worked furiously for an hour or two, then covered it, preparing to go to bed.

That night, for the first time in years, she felt compelled to lock her doors. That night, too, for the first time in years, David's face returned to her dreams. His grey eyes looked deeply into hers and his resonant voice, until now the only clear memory she had had, murmured, "Sweet lady . . . sweet lady . . ." over and over again.

When her alarm went off Eleanor reached out and slapped it angrily on the back of its noisy head, silencing it. She felt as if her head had just touched the pillow, as if she had never closed her eyes all night. She stumbled into the kitchen after a wash in cold water, and put her coffee on.

The sun was shining and she stepped outdoors to smell the early morning. The rose arbour was bathed in the golden glow of the new day and she walked to it, admiring the tender green shoots which covered it, and the dainty yellow buds with the dew still fresh upon them.

Eleanor looked down at the roots of the original bushes, the ones David had told her would never cover the arbour. She gasped, looked closer, spun and ran for the house.

She sank weakly to a chair in the kitchen, her eyes wide with fright. For there, in the mud from the rain a few days ago, had been big, booted footprints, pointing in the direction which showed her clearly that her sensation of the night before had not been nerves brought on by Grant's attempt to get her into his bed.

Someone had been looking at her! And

from the size of the prints, she knew it had not been Grant! Unbidden, the thought came to mind of the free-loader, if that was what he had been, who had headed toward the Anderson place, or the Exley's. But no . . . why would a stranger come and look in her windows? Maybe Bill had been around during the day when she was working and hadn't wanted to disturb her. Of course! That was it! She was just being foolish, letting her imagination run away with her.

Still, she reflected later, it wasn't that awful feeling of being stared at that had kept her awake all night, or most of it. That had been the direct result of Grant's insulting comment. Wondering if she could be frigid had made her remember David so vividly that she even dreamed of his face . . . No, she corrected herself, not his face, really . . . his eyes.

Well, if Grant is going to do that to me, then I'll never be able to forget enough to marry him. The best thing to do would be keep away from Grant for a while, to do a bit of soul-searching completely on her own.

With this in mind Eleanor sent her son off to school and walked up to the farm to use the telephone. She had never bothered to have a line brought down to the cottage. Grant was surprised by her call, and sounded cool and unforgiving. Though what he had to forgive her for she did not know! He put up no argument when she suggested they not see one another for a few weeks.

"O.K. by me," he said. "I'm trying to get a new motel opened up just outside of Kamloops, so I'll be up there for a while. I'll probably be back sometime in June . . . around the middle, I'd say. If you change your mind about us in the meantime, feel free to give me a call. I'll be in touch when I get back. So long, Ellie."

"So long, Grant."

So long, she repeated silently. So long and it didn't bother me a bit to say it . . . What's wrong with me that I don't care about Grant's going away, and going away mad, at that? He's been the only man in my life for the past four years, and for the three before that there was no one.

No one . . . save a ghost.

FOUR

A week had passed since Eleanor had said "So long" to Grant, and she had yet to feel that she missed him, or to feel any nearer a decision with regard to their future. She had worked hard during that week, and today Kathy was coming to spend the afternoon with her, sewing.

Eleanor sat on the back steps waiting for her friend, and a call made her raise her head, breaking into her thoughts. She stood and walked toward the glowing mother-to-be. "My goodness, Kath!" she exclaimed. "I've never seen anyone quite as pregnant as you are!" She took the bundle of pastel printed flannelette from Kathy. "Are you sure there's only one in there?"

Kathy sobered for an instant; she could only manage that long before her infectious grin broke out again. "Nope," she said cheerfully, "the doctor told me this morning he thinks we're doing a double on him!"

"You're kidding!" Eleanor gave the younger woman a hug. "Twins? He really thinks so?"

Kathy nodded and sat heavily on the cushion Eleanor had placed for her on the wooden bench in the arbour. "But the way I feel, it could be a colt. The way I look, too!" She folded her arms along the top of her protruding tummy and sighed. "All I know is that whatever it is, it had better hurry up and get here! I'm sick to death of waiting!"

"Oh-ho," jeered Eleanor gently. "Where's the girl who not so very long ago said she'd give it away if it came before the middle of June? Still more than two weeks to go, my pet."

"Don't remind me," groaned Kathy, pulling a face. She reached for another nightie which required a hem. "I really can't take much more of this, though, Ellie."

"I know. I remember," said Eleanor sympathetically. "Gosh, seven years ago. Is that all it's been? Sometimes it feels like forever, yet others, it seems like only yesterday. It's Phillip's birthday on Sunday, remember, and you and Bill are coming for dinner. There'll be a cake, with cherries in it," she added as an extra inducement.

"Oh, we'll be here. Wouldn't miss it for anything . . . except perhaps for my own 'whatever's' birthday. How goes the imaginary friend? Jeff, wasn't it? All forgotten, I imagine."

Eleanor rubbed her forehead with the back of her hand. "Oh, no. He's still very much in evidence. I have to send extra cookies and things out into the woods for Phil to share with 'Jeff'. Last week we had dinner at the motel with Grant, and 'Jeff' even shared our table, eating exactly what Phillip did. I have to say one thing for 'Jeff', though," she laughed. "He's a nice quiet guest. I didn't even know he was there until Phillip told me. And I even smiled at him!" she added in mockery of her son's words.

"My, how wonderful!" giggled Kathy. Then, "But speaking of Grant, which you haven't in the past few days, where is he? I haven't seen him around at all."

"Oh, he's gone to Kamloops to open up a new motel. He won't be back for a few weeks," replied Eleanor with an off-hand shrug. "How many pairs of sleepers have you made so far, Kath?" she asked, changing the subject.

The two talked of many things for the next couple of hours, and sewed industriously until Eleanor broke up the work by saying, "Want some iced tea?"

They left the shady arbour over which the buds of a week before had burst into a golden mass of perfumey blossoms which bobbled in the breeze in thick, short-stemmed clusters, attracting bees and hummingbirds.

In the cool kitchen Eleanor poured tea into tall, frosted glasses, added thin twists of lemon, placed the glasses on a tray with a plate of cookies and carried it all through to the living room. Kathy was sitting in an overstuffed chair, shoes off, her feet propped up on the coffee table. Her hands were clasped complacently over her belly, and she grinned at Eleanor.

"Don't mind, do you?"

"Of course not," Eleanor assured her friend. "You expectant mothers deserve a little pampering." She looked briefly wistful, Kathy thought. Almost envious of this enormous girth!

"Did you and Grant have a fight, Ellie?" she asked with sympathy.

"Sort of," Eleanor replied, still looking at Kathy's big tummy.

"Why don't you marry him? Then in no time at all you could look just like me!"

Eleanor laughed for a moment at the proudly pregnant girl, then sobered. She knew it was genuine interest in her welfare which prompted Kathy to ask such a personal question; friendship, not idle curiosity, and she replied in kind.

"I haven't agreed to marry him because I

don't think I love him enough. I'm not even sure he loves me, now, Kath." She went on to describe the happenings of the night of the dinner engagement the week before, and ended saying, "If he loved me, and didn't just want me, physically, he'd never have made that crack about my being frigid!"

"Oh, come on, now!" remonstrated Kathy. "Maybe the poor guy's just getting desperate. Lord knows he's hung around long enough for you to make up your mind sixteen times! What is it, four years?" At Eleanor's unhappy nod, she went on. "Well, after that long, even the most patient of suitors has a right to get a little bitter."

"But it's only been the last few months that I could have been said to be 'free', and even now I'm not . . . not legally, unless I have Dave declared dead."

"Are you going to?"

"I don't know, Kathy. I honestly don't know."

"Do you still hope he'll come back? Still love him that much?"

"I don't know that, either, Kath. But I do know that if he did come back, say today, he'd be a different man from the one who left me here, and I might not care for him at all. In fact, if he did come back, he'd have to have an awfully damned good reason for having stayed away so long or I wouldn't have a thing to do with him!"

"Well, I guess not!" exclaimed Kathy indignantly. "After all, a man can't just walk out for seven years and expect to come jaunting back whenever he feels like it!" She drained her glass and set it carefully on the floor beside her chair; the feet on the table, and the belly in her lap precluded her reaching the coffee table.

"More?" asked Eleanor, and at Kathy's pleased expression, rose and went to the kitchen to pour the tea. She let a gasp out of her, poked her head back through the door. "Hey!" she asked Kathy, "did you hear the school bus?"

"No. Why, is it late?"

"No! It's in!" She filled the two glasses and took them back, a frown on her face.

"Phillip's lunch kit and books are on the table, the cookie can has its lid off, and the little stinker's disappeared. Must be off in the woods again with his dear friend 'Jeff'. Oh, Kathy, I do wish he'd give up on that business!"

"Now, now. Just give him time, Ellie. He will give it up when he outgrows the need for it . . . having imaginary friends, I mean. Remember when it was Solomon the Soldier?"

Eleanor laughed at the memory. "Lord, yes! And woe betide any of us who referred to the fellow simply as Solomon! The whole title, or nothing at all." She sobered, frowning again, and said, "But this time it's different, somehow. He's making up the most intricate details about 'Jeff'. They began by cutting down the trees, clearing away the brush and laying the foundation logs. Now they're putting up walls. The way he talks about it is uncanny; almost as though he really were involved in building a log cabin. The work is going ahead at what seems a likely rate. You'd think he'd slip up once in a while and put in a window before building the wall, or something."

"Just shows the child has a level head on his shoulders. And," Kathy added, "that he has the same talent for making up stories as his mother does."

"Maybe," replied Eleanor doubtfully. "But I worry about him. Besides, I don't make up my stories; I just take the old legends which have existed for centuries and weave people into them."

"Could be that's what Phillip's doing. Perhaps he's following a story he's hearing from his teacher. She might be reading them a frontiertype book, chapter by chapter, and he's acting it out in his after-school play. But, look, Ellie, if you're really worried about him, why not walk over to where he's playing and sneak a look at him?"

"No!" yelped Eleanor sharply, then, seeing the astonished look on her friend's face, she went on more quietly. "Sorry, Kathy. I didn't mean to yell at you. But I stay this side of the creek. There are too many memories over there on the other side of the hill." Her eyes had a far-away look in them. "Too many ghosts . . ."

Kathy remained silent for a long time, not wanting to intrude on Eleanor's memories. She sipped at her tea, nibbled the slice of lemon, then said gently, "Maybe you should walk over there just once and see if you can lay those ghosts, Ellie. Maybe they are still there because you want them to be." When she received no reply, she rose clumsily to her feet. "I'm going to stagger off home, now," she said.

"I'll walk you home," offered Eleanor, pulling herself back with an effort from that far place and time she had been visiting.

"No need. I can make it," smiled Kathy.

"Not on your life! Now I know there's two babies waiting for their turn on earth, I'm going to look after you. After all," Eleanor grinned, pushing Kathy out of the house ahead of her, "who else has their own private army of one tank?"

The 'tank' laughed, and when the two women reached the farmhouse door Eleanor turned to go. "See you Sunday, love. Take care."

"Sunday . . . unless . . ." said Kathy wistfully.

"I'll keep my fingers crossed for you!"

When Phillip got off the school bus he walked slowly up the path toward home. He was feeling very, very blue. He had a note in his lunch kit from Miss Walker. She hadn't been going to give him one, but he had asked her why he didn't get one when all the other kids had. Miss Walker had got all red in the face and her eyes had got all shiny and she had said, "Phillip, dear, it's just a reminder to the fathers that tomorrow is the day they are going to get the sports field ready for race day."

"My mom could come!"

"No, Phillip. I'm afraid not. But your mom is making sandwiches for the picnic after the races on Monday, isn't she?"

"Yeah . . . but give me a note anyway, please Miss Walker. I'll give it to my friend, Jeff. He's building a log cabin and he's real strong and he could do more work than all those dumb old dads!"

Miss Walker sighed quietly and handed

Phillip a copy of the form letter.

On the bus, Jamie Peters, who was fat, and had a fat dad, too, had said, "Aw, you haven't got a dad to help with the field and I bet your old Jeff guy won't come either! I bet you haven't even got a friend named Jeff!"

"I have so! I have so! You wait! You ask your dad after Saturday and see what he says! My friend Jeff will so come and help!" reiterated Phillip heatedly.

"I can't ask my dad after Saturday 'cause he won't even be there! He's got better things to do; he has a golf game with his boss! I bet your old Jeff guy has better things planned, too!"

Maybe Jeff wouldn't go to the school to help! This hadn't occurred to Phillip before, but now it weighed heavily on his mind. He trudged slowly up the lane and into the house, creeping quietly. He didn't want to talk to his mother just yet.

He could hear his mom and Kathy talking in the living room, and he stood eavesdropping for a few minutes, putting off the time when he had to take the note to Jeff.

Soon, because the conversation in the living room wasn't all that interesting, just about his dad who hadn't come home, ever, he grabbed some cookies, took the note out of his lunch kit and went off to the other side of the hill.

Panting, he came to a halt beside Jeff who grinned down at him and said, "Hi, sport!"

"Jeff! Jeff! Will you go to the school on Saturday . . . tomorrow . . . and help with the sports field for race day on Monday? The teacher wasn't going to give me a note because I haven't got a dad and my mom said that even if he did come back he'd have to have an awful . . . she said a bad word . . . good reason for staying away so long and so I haven't got a dad to go and I told Miss Walker you would go and she gave me the note!" He sucked in a long breath and pushed the note at Jeff. "I told her you were strong and could build a log cabin and do more work than the other dads!" His wide grey eyes looked up at Jeff with faith and trust and hope.

Jeff read the note which was addressed to "Dear Fathers", folded it small and tucked it away in his shirt pocket. He hunkered down beside the boy and said, "Sport, why don't you ask Grant?"

"Oh, Grant wouldn't do anything like that! Besides, he's gone away!" The light in Phillip's eyes showed that this was to be treated as good news. "My mom said he won't be back for weeks. Hey, Jeff, what's

79

frigid? Grant said that to Mom and she didn't even say goodnight to him. Is that a bad word?"

Jeff smiled. "No, Phil. Not really, but it would be sure to make your mom mad." His smile turned into a grin, as if he were amused at some secret joke. He rumpled the hair of the boy beside him. "Tell you what . . . I'll go to the school tomorrow, and if I see Miss Walker I'll tell her you sent me. O.K.?"

Phillip beamed. "O.K.!" Then, obviously thinking that if favours were being bestowed, it was up to him to do a little bestowing himself, he said, "Sunday's my birthday, Jeff. Will you come to dinner?"

Jeff looked sadly at his companion. "Son," he said slowly, "I'd like nothing better than to come to dinner on your birthday, but I bet your mom has already planned on the number of guests she's having. One more might upset all her plans, and then where'd we be?"

"But there's still time to ask her, and she could cook a bigger cake," Phillip replied earnestly, adding, "Anyway, it's only Kathy and Bill coming."

Jeff, who by this time knew of Kathy and Bill and their place in the scheme of Phillip's life, said, "No friends from school?"

80

"Naw . . . they all live too far away except for Jamie Peters and I don't like him. He's a dumb old fatty. His dad's fat, too, and he isn't even going to help get the field ready!"

The triumph inherent in Phillip's tones made Jeff smile. "It's not very nice to dislike someone just because they're fat, Phil. He can't help it, can he now?"

"Aw . . . that's what Mom says!"

"And you listen to your mother, young 'un! But I promise I will help get the field ready, so you don't have to worry about that any more."

"Will you come to my party?"

"No, son." That was the final answer, and Phillip knew it. "What do you want for your birthday, Phil? A pony, maybe?"

"No! Ponies is horses but smaller and I don't like horses!"

"Don't you? That's too bad. I'm getting a horse next week and I was hoping you and I could ride together sometimes."

"No! That day I laughed at Grant when he fell off he put me on his horse and it was so big! Bill took me down and I ran and ran in the woods and then I found an axe and I pretended I was chopping off Grant's head and things and . . ." Phillip broke off abruptly, remembering just whose axe it was he had found and used. "Oh!" he said, putting his hand to his mouth, waiting for Jeff to get mad at him for doing such a bad thing as chopping someone up, even if it was only pretend.

Jeff did not get mad. "I understand, Phil. You said you hated him, and just then, you did. It's all right to hate someone sometimes, but you just have to learn not to go around chopping them up. You chopped a log, and then we started building the cabin together and you forgot all about hating Grant, didn't you?"

"Mostly . . . but I hated him before that, when I was just little and he laughed every time I cried when I hurt myself . . . and when he tried to give me riding lessons. He called me a little baby."

"Oh. Well, son, sometimes even grownups can be wrong. You're not a little baby at all. It takes a really big boy to help build a log cabin." The firm conviction in Jeff's words made Phillip glow with pleasure.

"Did you ever hate anybody enough to want to chop on them, Jeff?" asked Phillip, frowning slightly, still not sure that it was all right to hate.

"Yes. Once."

"Who?"

"Someone you wouldn't know about, Phil."

"What did you do? Chop him?"

"No. I told you, we might hate people now and then, but we don't chop them up. Anyway, when I found out what he had done to me, he was already dead." Jeff looked incredibly sad and Phillip slipped a hand into the big one hanging by Jeff's side. The man looked down at the child's anxious face. "It's O.K. I got over hating him. I can understand why he did what he did to me, and I can forgive him, I think. But it's not my forgiveness I worry about . . ."

Phillip, who hadn't a clue what Jeff was talking about, said, "How come you have whiskers now?" Jeff had been clean-shaven that day when they had first met, and the boy couldn't have said when the change had taken place . . .

"I felt like growing a beard," smiled Jeff, glad the other topic had been dropped. "Like it?" He stroked the short, yet full covering over his lower face.

Phillip nodded slowly. "Um . . . yes," he decided. "I like it!"

"Good. What should I get you for your birthday?"

"Gee, I don't know! What do you want to give me?" he countered.

"Something I can't . . . but how'd you like a lucky horse-shoe to hang over your door?"

"Oh, sure!" Phillip's eyes glowed. Had Jeff offered him a stale, cooked carrot for his birthday, that too would have been just as good. "But could I wait for it until we finish the cabin and hang it over our door?"

"If that's what you want to do, of course. Now I think you've stayed long enough. Your mom will be worried. See you tomorrow? When I get back from helping with the field?"

"Yup. See you, Jeff."

The morning of Phillip's birthday brought low-lying clouds and heavy rain. Both he and his mother slept late, due, no doubt, to the dark skies, and when she awoke Eleanor went to the back porch at once to see if the basket was there as Ralph Exley had promised. It was, and she lifted the lid to be met by a shiny black nose, a whimpering sound and the scrabbling of little paws against the wicker.

"Oh, you are a darling!" she crooned, scooping the pup onto her lap. "Come and meet your new master."

She carried the puppy into Phillip's room, put it on the bed beside her son's head and stood back. The pup sniffed, licked then sneezed. Phillip opened his eyes a crack, then widened them into big, grey orbs. He squeezed them shut for a moment before he popped them open wider still.

"Wow!" he said. Then "Wow!" again.

"Happy birthday, love," smiled Eleanor. "Like him?"

Phillip's expression was answer enough, but he said, "Oh, Mom! What is he?"

"Black Labrador retriever," replied Eleanor.

Phillip squirmed to get away from the wet little tongue which was trying to wash his chin. "Will he get big?"

"Pretty big. Like this, maybe," said his mother, indicating height with her hand.

"Wow!" said Phillip once more. "Can I go show him to Jeff before breakfast?"

"No, darling," chuckled Eleanor. "It's pouring rain and he's too little to go running through the woods yet. You'll have to stay home with him and help him learn all sorts of things. I'm sure Jeff will understand."

"Then can I go tell Jeff about him?"

"Not in the rain! And if you want your puppy to really be yours, you'll have to stay out of the woods until he's big enough to go along. You'll have to spend lots and lots of time with him in case he thinks he's my dog, not yours, because I'll have to look after him when you're in school. What are you going to name him?"

"Casey," replied Phillip without an instant's hesitation, looking surprised at his mother's question.

"Casey? Why?"

" 'Cause that's his name, Mom. That's what you just called him."

"I did?" said Eleanor, who knew quite well she had done nothing of the sort.

"Yes. You said, 'Casey thinks he's my dog'." Phillip frowned and held the puppy closer to him for a moment. "How come he thinks he's your dog, Mom?" He was quite aggrieved at the thought.

"Phillip! I don't believe you heard a word I said! I did not say 'Casey thinks he's my dog', I said, 'IN case he thinks he's my dog'."

"Yes," said Phillip, agreeably. "That's what you said, Mom . . . 'Casey thinks he's your dog', and you said I couldn't go to Jeff's 'cause it's raining and . . ."

"All right! All right!" Eleanor laughed, holding up her hands to ward off the spate of words she expected to hear pouring out of her son as he repeated their previous conversation verbatim . . . as he had heard it. "Breakfast! Let's go!"

. . . But 'Casey' . . . the dog remained.

The supper party went off well, with everyone, including the still-pregnant Kathy batting balloons wildly around the house while the puppy barked shrilly, getting in the way, and getting too excited, Eleanor declared, wiping up the third puddle in five minutes.

"Put him on the back porch, darling. His basket's there. He'll be warm enough!" she added, seeing the mutinous look on Phillip's face. "And then you'd better get ready for bed. Big day tomorrow, don't forget. I'll be there to see you win lots and lots of races . . . or at least try hard."

"Jeff," Phillip informed the party of adults, in an attempt to gain time out of bed, "went to the school to help the dads get the field ready. He told me last night. But," he added sadly, "Miss Walker wasn't there, so he couldn't tell her he was my friend. Will you tell her tomorrow, Mom? Please? And tell her him and me's building a log cabin?"

"Oh, Phillip! If I tell Miss Walker anything, it will be about your grammar! Let's not talk about 'Jeff' right now. You're only stalling. Put the puppy out now and say goodnight. I'll come and tuck you in soon."

After she had tucked Phillip into his bed Eleanor returned to her guests. "Well, Bill, I hope you're right, and having the pup will keep him home. I don't know why I didn't have sense enough to think of something like that myself!"

"Probably because you were never a little boy," said Bill, with admirable logic. "That's where I think single parents have it rough with a child of the opposite sex; they can't see things quite the same way as a parent of the same sex can, not one with a half-decent memory of his or her own childhood, that is. Your old dad must have had a few problems raising you, Ellie, what with being a man raising a girl, and a double dose of the 'generation gap', as well."

"If he did, I was blissfully unaware," she responded. "At least until he tried to tell me about my rapidly approaching puberty." She grinned, remembering. "There, we did have a few hang-ups. I sure hope you're still around then, Bill, when Phillip starts to grow up. I'll need all the help I can get!"

"That's a ways off yet," said Kathy, making no attempt to hide her prodigious yawn. "Before you have to worry about that, you'll be all settled down and married to someone . . . Grant, likely, and can sit back and leave it all to him."

But will I have? Eleanor asked herself later that night as she lay sleepless in her bed. Will I ever settle down and marry Grant? She tried to picture him beside her, tousled with love and sleep and the only thing she could see was David's eyes, looking deeply into hers, and the memory of him flooded over her again; the sound of his voice seemed to fill her ears and she sat up, holding her hands to her head, moaning.

Why won't he go away and stop haunting me? Why can't I be sensible and forget him? And the answer came to her immediately: Because I still want him! I still need these memories, and until I no longer have need for them they will remain, just as Phillip will keep his imaginary friends until he outgrows the need for them.

Oh, David, what has your disappearance done to me, and what has my lack of acceptance, my failure to adjust to it, done to our son?

FIVE

Race day at the school was a thunderous success. Kids ran whooping in droves, powered, it seemed, by so many small, noisy piston-driven engines. The amount of energy expended would have lit the towns' combined lights for two weeks, Eleanor thought as she sat behind a long trestle table preparing to serve plates of sandwiches and potato salad to the assembled adults. The kids, those who were not running wildly about, were hovering hungrily near a large vat of wieners simmering on a portable stove.

Further down the table from her, other mothers were slicing meat, while others still cut pies and cakes. The abundance of food would never be eaten, Eleanor decided, looking at the hams, cold turkeys and roasts of beef in the section next to her own of green salads, potato salads and sandwiches, and at the amount of desserts at the far end of the table.

The racing was finished. Phillip's team had won the tug-o'-war, with chubby little Jamie Peters as anchor man, and for once, she was pleased to note, the poor child was not being treated as a pariah by his school mates, her son among them.

Phillip came galloping up just then, his one blue, two red and three white ribbons fluttering on his grubby tee-shirt, a wide grin splitting his equally grubby face. He glanced around to see if anyone were near, then whispered to his mother, "Did you see him, Mom?"

"Who, dear?"

"Jeff! He was over by the back-stop when we won the tug-o'-war and when I ran over to say 'Hi', he left." Phillip showed no disappointment at this development, naturally, his mother decided, admiring the way Phillip could go on making up reasons for never having Jeff show himself when there were others present. Phillip burbled on, "But that's O.K., though, 'cause he's afraid to be around me when there's other people here, 'cause he might forget and tell my secret. I told him about . . ." And Phillip leaned closer still, his steamy breath tickling in Eleanor's ear ". . . Lorna!"

Dear Diary, thought Eleanor, a smile twitching at the corners of her mouth. "I'm glad you like him enough to tell him about that," she said, giving her son a hug.

"Oh, I don't just like him, Mom," said

Phillip confidingly, "I love him like you only different. Can I have a hot-dog now, Mr. Exley?" This last was bellowed at the top of his lungs as he roared away to the cooking pot presided over by Ralph Exley, the neighbour who had provided the puppy for his birthday.

At length the trestle table held only scraps and crumbs; the miracle had happened and all the food had vanished. The adults, exhausted, crumpled in heaps on blankets on the grass. Not so the children, who, stuffed as they were with hot-dogs, cakes and pies, to say nothing of quarts and quarts of ice cream, seemed only to have been recharged.

Eleanor sank back on her blanket and propped herself on one elbow to watch the crowning of the May Queen. The "throne" was set in a beautiful little bower made of lilacs and maple leaves, yellow broom and hyacinths interspersed with the white stars of dogwood flowers.

The parade began with little boys riding on decorated bicycles in the lead of the "Princesses", small girls gowned in long, pastel organdies, carrying small baskets of petals which were tossed by handsful along the path to be taken by the May Queen. A cheer went up from the children as she came around the corner of the school, walking with extreme dignity in her long, white gown. The picture of decorum, she glided toward the bower where she was to be crowned with a garland of spring flowers, and upon reaching the two shallow steps which led to her throne, she raised a laugh by turning and calling loudly, "See Daddy? I didn't trip on my own big feet!" and immediately tripping on the hem of her gown as she mounted the steps.

Later, driving home with the evening sun in her eyes, Eleanor rubbed a hand across her forehead which was aching slightly from too much sun, too much food and most certainly from too much noise. Phillip leaned forward and spoke in her right ear. "Wasn't she pretty, Mom?"

"Um-hmm," she replied, wishing he didn't have to be so loud. "Sit down and do up your seat belt." Eleanor knew her son was referring to Lorna, the princess in pale gold.

They were greeted at home by an ecstatic Casey who forgave them at once for leaving him, and showed his magnanimity by producing a puddle on the floor. Eleanor bent over to mop up and arose feeling sick and dizzy.

Neither she nor Phillip felt like eating after the excesses of the day, so Eleanor took a couple of aspirins and went into the coolness of the rose arbour to rest for an hour before Phillip's bed time. The hour did her no good at all. She wished her head would quit aching, but it just seemed to be getting worse. Not only that, but her sinuses were stuffed up. Maybe we'll have a storm, she thought, looking with apathetic eyes at an unrelentingly blue dome of sky which remained cloudless and bright even at seven o'clock in the evening. She rose and called Phillip to get ready for bed.

He put the pup into its basket and went with great reluctance to have his bath. When he was finished, he appeared before his mother, scrubbed and pink, shining with good health and over-abundant energy. It made Eleanor tired just to look at him.

"I'm not tired, Mom. Can't I stay up just a bit longer?" he wheedled.

"No. Maybe you're not tired, but I am. It's nearly eight now, so let's get going, young man!" She led him off to his bed, read him an extremely brief story and kissed him. "Goodnight, darling."

" 'Night, Mom." Phillip, who was not tired, yawned. "How come I have to go to bed when you're tired?"

"Just the way life is, Phil."

"Aw, that's no answer. I'll ask Jeff when I see him again. He always gives me good answers . . . 'cept once . . .'" and Eleanor decided her son was about to ask another question, so she quickly flicked off the light and left her son still wondering what 'frigid' meant. She had been too beat to ask him what question 'Jeff' had answered less than satisfactorily.

For the next four days Eleanor fought the symptoms of her cold, taking pills and just managing to keep going. Phillip would come home from school, play rambunctiously with Casey for a little while, then hare off into the woods, leaving the puppy sleeping peacefully in his basket.

Eleanor felt too miserable to try to keep her active, noisy little son around. She knew it was a cop-out, but it was so much easier to let him go. At least then it was quiet for her poor, aching head. Phillip, too, seemed to have developed a new sense of responsibility since the advent of the puppy. Instead of her having to call him every night, she was delighted to find him home on time for supper, ready and willing to feed his pet. Even if that's all the puppy's done for me, he's well worth it, she decided.

"I'm glad you're coming home on time, now, Phil," she told him one night when she was tucking him into bed. "It's much easier for me this way."

"That's what Jeff said," Phillip informed her seriously. "He says now that I have someone small and helpless relying on me . . . he meant Casey . . . I have to watch the time."

"I'm so glad, dear," said Eleanor, trying not to smile. Not for the world would Phillip admit that he, himself had decided to begin behaving with a more responsible attitude. Far easier to say that the ubiquitous 'Jeff' was responsible. That way, any back-sliding could be blamed on 'Jeff', too.

Oddly enough, even though he was still spending much time in the forest, after that one mention of Jeff, Phillip seemed to forget about him. He would go out, return muddy or dusty, according to weather conditions, but with a silence on the subject of his playmate which gave his mother an easier mind.

Perhaps, she decided, the woods are simply a good place to play for their own sake, and no 'friend' with a log cabin is necessary.

That was not true.

The day after the races at school, Phillip went barrelling into the woods, calling loudly as he rushed into the clearing. "Jeff! Jeff! I saw you!" He fell into a panting heap beside Jeff, who was making what appeared to be a lean-to shed out of poles. "Did you see me win the tug-o'-war?"

"Sure did, sport! Saw your team win second prize in the relay race, too. Nice going! How was your birthday?"

"Great! Hey, Jeff, guess what my mom gave me!"

"What?" Jeff smiled down into the glowing little face.

"Guess!" Phillip hugged himself in ecstacy, bouncing from one foot to the other. "You'll never guess!"

Jeff pondered, then said, "A new pair of pants? . . . A bike? . . . A sled?" And at each wrong answer the little boy shook his head, his shaggy hair flying around his face, his eyes dancing with delight. At last he could stand the guessing game no longer.

"A puppy!" he blurted. "A little bitty puppy what's going to grow up to be this big!" He indicated, as his mother had done, only adding a foot or two of exaggeration.

"A black Labrador retriever called Casey!"

Jeff opened his eyes wide, showing astonishment. "No!" he said, "not a real live puppy of your very own?"

"Yup!" Phillip nodded earnestly. "Honest, Jeff. But he can be yours, too, if you like. He c'n b'long to both of us and to Mom, too, of course. Mom says he's too little to go running through the woods and I have to stay home and look after him until he's growed up some, but she let me come today 'cause she doesn't feel good and my racket hurts her head."

"Well, we'll have to make sure you're home on time to feed your pup, Phil. If your mom has a headache she won't want to have to go outside to call you."

"What's that you're building now, Jeff?"

"A lean-to."

"What's it for?"

"Siwash."

"Who's that?"

"My horse."

Phillip backed up a pace or two. He raised big, hurt eyes to Jeff. "A horse?" He looked betrayed; his lower lip trembled slightly.

Jeff nodded, leaning another pole against the cross beam and nailing it in place. "I told you I was getting one."

Phillip looked around apprehensively, "Is it here?"

Again Jeff nodded, not stopping his work. "In a horse trailer over behind the truck. Let me have a nail, please, Phil. I have to get this finished so I can bed him down for the night."

Phillip handed over a nail. "Horses don't have beds!" he said derisively.

"No," replied Jeff agreeably and evenly, "they have stables. Every creature likes to have a warm, dry place to sleep, out of the wind, out of the rain. Siwash will like to have this shed we're making for him, where he can eat his oats and sleep warm. You wouldn't enjoy sleeping standing up in a trailer, would you?"

"No-o-o, I guess not," said the child doubtfully. "Will you still like me when he comes here to sleep in his shed?"

"Of course, son. You have Casey, and you still like me, don't you?"

"Yes. You don't want me to get up on him, do you?"

"No. Not unless you want to. May I have some more nails, please?"

The following afternoon when Phillip arrived the lean-to had been completed. It was roofed with shakes over the frame-work of poles, and the front, too, had been covered with shakes, leaving an opening in one side in which Jeff hid hung a Dutch door made of poles and hinged with leather. The top of the door was open, and from it protruded the head and neck of an enormous looking horse with a calm, sleepy demeanor.

Phillip stood well back, watching the horse with distrustful eyes. Jeff came quietly up behind him and when he touched Phillip's shoulder the boy squealed and jumped. "Easy, son. Easy. It's only me," said Jeff in his calm, resonant voice. "See? That's Siwash, and he's all locked up in there, poor old thing, because I knew you were coming."

The horse whickered softly, tossing his head and Jeff went on in the same even tones, his hand still comfortingly warm on Phillip's shoulder. "He's asking for an apple. Get me one out of that basket over there, will you?"

Phillip tip-toed to the bushed basket of apples, selected one by feel alone, not taking his eyes off the horse and sneaked in a wide arc around, back to Jeff. The man took the apple and went alone to the horse.

He held it out while Phillip watched from a safe distance, and the large, yellowish teeth snaffled it daintily from his outstretched palm. Siwash chomped noisily, tossed his head and made a sound. "No, Si. Sorry boy. That's enough for now. When my friend's gone home for his dinner, I'll let you out. I know you hate being penned up in there, but you see, he's been my friend longer than you have, and he's a little worried that you and he might not get along together." The horse snorted gently, blowing his warm breath over the side of Jeff's head, ruffling his hair and beard.

Jeff went right on talking, after pausing politely to listen while the horse made his sounds. "No, no. Don't say that! Of course he's not afraid of you. He's just had a couple of bad experiences with horses, and he worries a bit."

Phillip edged just a step or two closer. "Are you and that horse really talking to each other?" he wanted to know.

As if on cue, the horse whickered and Jeff smiled. "We are indeed," he said to Phillip, then turning once more to the horse, he said, "Well, all right, my friend. Just one more." Again the horse spoke and tossed his head. "Oh, Si, I don't know," replied Jeff doubtfully, "but if you think it'll make you feel happier about staying inside on such a nice afternoon, I'll ask him. Just to prove that he doesn't really hate you." As Jeff turned from the lean-to, the horse muttered something quietly. "Hey, now! Do you think so? I'll try that!" Jeff replied, sounding impressed.

"Phillip," he said, reaching into the basket for an apple, "as you heard Siwash telling me, he's feeling badly about your not liking him very much. I told him that you like him all right . . . aren't scared of him, and he says that just to prove it, if you'd give him an apple, he'd feel better. Now, ordinarily I would never give him another this close to supper time, but just this once, because he's sad, I've agreed. Take this over to him, will you, please?"

Jeff held out the apple to the boy who backed away, his face going pale. "No! I don't want to! He's too big!"

"Steady, now," said Jeff. "That's what Si thought you'd say. He's smarter than I thought he was. He suggested that maybe if I picked you up and held you while you fed him the apple, he wouldn't look so big to you. Want to try it that way?"

"NO! NO!"

"O.K., Phil. No need to shout. He understands, don't you Si?"

The horse answered softly and withdrew his head and neck.

"I have your birthday present here, Phillip," Jeff told the child, giving him a warm hug around the shoulders. "I couldn't find one in any of the stores I went to, but Siwash had an extra one. He said I could

102

give it to you. It's from both of us. Like it?"

Phillip took the heavy horse-shoe in two hands and smiled up at Jeff, his eyes aglow, partly from having the gift, and partly from the knowledge that even if he didn't want to go too close to Siwash, Jeff was not going to say he was a sissy. "Sure I like it! Come on Jeff. Let's get the cabin finished so we can hang it up!"

Presently Phillip said, "What time is it, Jeff? I have to feed Casey at five-thirty."

"Twenty after, sport, so you'd better make tracks. See you tomorrow?"

"Yup. Tomorrow, Jeff."

When Phillip entered the clearing the next afternoon, the door to the stable stood open and neither Jeff nor the horse were to be seen.

Much work had been done on the cabin; the ridge pole was erected and rafters had been strung across the opening between gable ends. A pile of cedar shakes stood on the ground, waiting to become a roof. Phillip stood looking at the cabin, wishing he didn't have to go to school. There was so much going on that he had to miss! He heard the gentle clip-clop of Siwash's hooves and leapt through the doorway to be safe until the horse had been locked up in his stall. He heard Jeff talking to his mount.

"Here we are, boy, home again." Jeff gave no sign that he had spotted the brief flash of movement when Phillip had darted into the cabin. "No, sorry, Si. You have to go inside. You know Phillip'll be here soon, and he'd rather not see you wandering all around the clearing. Now, Si! Don't cry about it. Oh, come on now! You know I'll give you an apple to make up for locking you in like a prisoner."

When the bottom half of the Dutch door had been securely latched, Phillip came out of the cabin. He walked over to the bushel basket of apples, selected one which he took to Jeff. He turned as if surprised to see the boy, and took the apple with a smile of thanks and fed it to the horse. Siwash chomped with vigor for a moment, swallowed noisily and looked around for more. Phillip gave Jeff a pleading glance and asked, "Can't he have just one more? It won't spoil his dinner."

Jeff walked casually away. "He could, I guess, but I don't have time to give it to him. Have to get this roof put on. Might rain any day now." He climbed a ladder and began hammering shakes onto the lower edge of the roof.

Phillip stood torn between his feelings of guilt that the horse had to be imprisoned and his fear of approaching it with an appeasement.

Out of the corner of his eye Jeff saw guilt begin to take the upper hand. He backed silently down the ladder, yet seemed unaware of Phillip's halting progress toward the horse. However, when the child was but two short paces away and Siwash whinnied, Jeff was ready to catch the cannon-ball of boy who ran to him, yelling.

Jeff held the shaking little body close for a minute then stood, the child still in his arms. "Come on, son. Like Si said yesterday, if I hold you up, he won't look so big. O.K.?"

Phillip drew in a long, shuddering breath and clung to the back of Jeff's collar. "O.K., but I still don't like him much. I just feel sorry that he's locked up. Maybe another apple will make him happier."

"Hold it on the flat of your hand and don't let those big teeth worry you. Horses never eat people. All they eat are oats and hay and apples and sometimes sugar, but that's not good for them." He talked gently and approached the horse slowly.

When he was within an arm's length of Siwash, Phillip held out the apple on a shaking hand. The horse took it gently and munched, drops of juice splattering from

105

his jaws. He whinnied softly and Jeff whispered to Phillip, "Say, 'You're welcome, Si,' . . . he was thanking you."

Obediently, Phillip said, "You're welcome, Si."

Thursday and Friday afternoons were just about exact repeats of Wednesday; Siwash was locked up with many loud apologies from Jeff and given an extra apple by Phillip, for the inconvenience.

Then came Saturday . . .

Saturday morning was sunny and bright, a perfect June morning and Eleanor woke with her head feeling worse than ever. It was totally stuffed up and her chest ached, too. Her vision swam as she sat up and she held her head in her hands until she felt it settle down a bit. Phillip was in his room, with Casey in bed, she judged from the sounds of merriment pouring forth.

Oh, these summer colds, she lamented. They hang on for ever and ever! She sneezed and climbed wearily from her bed. How am I going to get through the weekend with Phillip home all day? she wondered. If I didn't feel too terrible. I'd get in the car and go see the doctor. I should ask Bill to take me, but Kathy's due any day now, and I'd hate to take Bill away . . . But she did feel too terrible, so she dropped the idea of seeing the doctor, and instead sat slumped at the table drinking tasteless coffee and nibbling at sawdust-toast while her son packed in two bowls of cereal, a boiled egg and an orange.

"Mom!" called Phillip loudly from two feet away, with his mouth full of half-chewed orange, "Can I take Casey into the woods today?" At her grimace of pain, which Phillip took to be the forerunner of a refusal, he added, "To play with Jeff. He'd like to see him, Mom, I know he would! Huh, Mom? Huh?"

"Phillip, don't yell! My head hurts. I told you . . . he's too small yet to walk all that way."

"I'll carry him, Mom, honest I will, all the way there, and all the way back. There's lots of room for him to play in the clearing now, it's big. It used to be just a little place, Mom, with a dogwood tree at the edge, but now the dogwood's right out in the middle and the cabin's just beside it, so there's lots of room and he won't get lost!"

A little clearing with a dogwood at one edge, Eleanor thought agonizedly. So that's his favourite place to play. I might have known! Then quickly, before he could shatter her skull and before she began to shed the tears which she knew were close, Eleanor said, "Go ahead, son. But look after Casey and be home for lunch."

"Can I pack a lunch? Can I, Mom? Huh?"

"No!" And Phillip scooped up his pup and scrammed. When he was out of sight, Eleanor let the despair and desolation wash over her. The clearing, as Phillip called it; her glade. The place where her love had first found her, the place where her child had been conceived; her special place had been taken over by a small, noisy boy, a puppy and an imaginary playmate. Something in her mind told her to think about it for a minute or two . . . something Phillip had said needed consideration, but her mind refused to function, and she never did get to wondering about how one small boy could have made a glade grow into a clearing where the tree from the edge now stood near the middle . . .

Eleanor put her head down in her arms right there in the mess and crumbs from breakfast and wept.

"I'm so lonely," she sobbed to herself. "How much more of this loneliness can I endure?" As she wept, she did not hear the screen door squeak open, and the first inkling she had that she was not alone was when a muffled gasp sounded just as two arms slipped around her and her head was pulled onto a masculine chest.

"What's the trouble, Ellie?" asked Grant. "I found I couldn't stay away and wait for you to call me, so I came back. Just in time, too, it seems. Don't cry, Ellie. What is it? Did you miss me?"

"Oh, Grant! Yes!"

SIX

"Yes, yes, Grant!" she sobbed against his chest. "I must have been missing you! I feel so miserable . . . My head aches, I hurt all over and my sinuses are all plugged up. Oh, Grant, I'm so lonely!" He let her cry for a few more minutes, holding her until she tried to push away from him, saying, "Oh, God, I'm so sick!"

He touched her forehead and stepped back a half pace. "You have a bit of fever, Ellie. I hope you're not coming down with anything serious." The concern in his tone made her fall apart all over again, and she buried her head against him.

"Hold me, Grant! Oh, please just hold me and let me lean on you for a little while. I've been trying to keep going for Phillip's sake, and now I'm just too tired and miserable to go on!"

He held her, rocking her gently, and the comfort she found in his arms was enormous. She pushed down the nasty little voice which told her she would have been just as comforted if Bill, or the mail-man or

110

the garbage man had been the one in whose arms she was sheltering. It was just so good to be held like this, to know there was one other person in the world who cared if she lived or died, and nasty little voices notwithstanding, she needed someone . . . Grant . . . ! right now.

"Don't be lonely any more, Ellie," said Grant. "Don't keep yourself in a position where you have no one to help you when you're sick and can't go on. Lean on me, darling. Let me take over today and everyday. I need you, too Ellie, and you need me. Admit it! Start the proceedings! Do it now!"

Eleanor shuddered once, then in capitulation, slumped against him, knowing that if she hadn't been so sick, so weak, she would have refused. But she was sick, was weak, and he was here, warm, and real and loving her, asking for her love, for the right to protect her, help her, and she raised her face to his, saying, "All right, Grant. I will. I will, and I'll try to be a good wife to you. You know my love won't be all yours, ever, but if you can accept that, accept what I can give you and not ask for everything, then I'll start proceedings and marry you as soon as possible."

"I'll accept what you can give me, Ellie,

but I don't believe you'll never love me fully. You will! I'll teach you to. I'll make you forget him and you'll never have any regrets." He cuddled her closely for another moment then lifted her to her feet.

"Come on, you go lie down and I'll clean up in here." He helped her tenderly to her room and when he would have unbuttoned her housecoat, exposing her flimsy nightie, she stayed his hands.

"No! No, I'll keep it on. I'm cold, Grant."

Dimly, Eleanor heard the rattle of dishes, the hum of the vacuum cleaner over the carpet in hallway and living room. She could hear the sounds of doors opening and closing and knew Grant was picking things up, putting them away, tidying the house. The knowledge that when she did feel like getting up, she would do so to a clean house, was comforting. She dozed until he brought her a cup of tea.

"It's so nice to be looked after," she said, giving him a sleepy smile and then sneezing, slopping the tea into the saucer. Grant snatched it from her as she wound up for another sneeze and put it on the bedside table. He sat down in the chair near her bed and looked around complacently.

"This is the first time I've actually been in this room, Ellie. I like it. Should we keep the cottage for odd weekends when we want to get away?"

Something in her recoiled at the thought of Grant sharing this room, this bed with her. "I . . . I . . . don't know, Grant. Would you want to stay here?"

"Sure," he said, seemingly surprised at the hesitation she was showing. "Why not?"

Why not indeed? she asked silently. Is he really so insensitive that he doesn't know why not? "No . . . no good reason, I guess, Grant . . . I just thought . . . you'd prefer a different place."

"Heck no! Here, drink your tea. This cottage is as good a place as any. But there is one thing I want to do, Ellie, and that is get rid of the Robins. This set-up you have with them is ridiculous! What we'll do is have a resident manager, pay him a salary and reap the profits of the farm for ourselves! How you ever came to that stupid arrangement with him in the first place, is something I don't understand. But no woman," he added kindly, "should be expected to have much business sense."

Eleanor felt her hackles rise, felt her nostrils begin to flare, tried and failed to control herself. "It's a damned good agreement I have with Kathy and Bill! It works out well for all of us! Bill pays me an excellent rent

113

for the use of both house and land, and you have to admit that, as long as a man is working a farm for himself, he puts more into it than he would if he were just on salary. I want this place cared for properly for Phillip's sake! It will be his one day, if he wants it, and if he doesn't, as seems likely, the way Bill is looking after it it's going to have a great resale value!"

"But you don't understand the financial end of it, dear," explained Grant with great patience. "Do you get any more rent from him if the yield is particularly good, or milk prices go up in any given year?"

"Maybe not," she responded tiredly, "But on the other hand, when the year is a bad one, I don't get less, either."

The weariness in her voice must have tweaked a nerve of contrition in Grant's soul, for he patted her knees which were humped up under her covers and said, "Ellie, let me make all these decisions for you in the future. You're tired of all this, and you need me to do it for you. I want to look after you. You know that, don't you?"

"Yes, Grant . . . I know it."

"Then couldn't you try to look a little happier about our engagement?" he asked wistfully.

Eleanor forced a weak smile. Never had

she felt less like looking happy! They weren't even engaged, not really, anyway, and already Grant was trying to run things his way, trying to get rid of her tenants, her friends! "But we aren't engaged Grant," she protested. "Not yet. We can't be. I have to see a lawyer first, and when all the arrangements have been made, when I'm free . . ." She broke off while a racking cough shook her, and took notice of the fact that Grant leaned well back in his chair while she spewed germs forth. Irrationally, she felt hurt that he was afraid of catching something from her, even though she had always known Grant's dread of illness. Why should it bother her now?

When the coughing spasm had ended, Grant started to speak, but Eleanor forestalled him, waving a hand for silence. "If you'll just be patient a little longer, Grant, then I'll become engaged to you and we'll tell the whole world! Can't you see that it would be wrong to make any kind of announcement while I'm still legally married to David? Let me tie up those loose ends first, and then we can shout it from the rooftops and I'll start wearing that enormous rock you offered me last Christmas." She gave him a sweet smile as she finished speaking, and he must have been mollified

115

for he leaned nearer and stroked her hair.

"Good!" he said softly yet triumphantly. "Now I'm going to make some lunch for you and you are going to eat every bit of it! Where's the kid?"

"Phillip," she said, deliberately stressing her son's name, "is out in the woods playing. He has a puppy. I got it from Ralph Exley for Phil's birthday. He'll be back soon. Lately he's had a built-in clock and comes home on time to feed Casey."

"Casey being the dog?" said Grant coldly.

"Yes," she nodded. "He's a cute pup, Grant. You'll like him."

"Not bloody likely!" he snapped. "Dogs aren't my thing at all! You know that, Ellie! He'd better not get too attached to it, because dogs don't belong in motels. They're dirty, noisy and they frighten the guests!"

"Grant! You can't expect me to make him give . . ." Eleanor broke off as she heard the slam of the screen door, the pounding of footsteps across the kitchen floor which heralded Phillip's arrival. "Hey, Mom? Where are you?"

Before Eleanor could answer, Grant stepped out of the room, pulling the door closed behind him. "Shut up!" Eleanor heard him snarl. "Don't you know your mother's sick? All this racket isn't going to make her feel any better! Get that mutt out of here, too. I just finished vacuuming the hall . . ."

Grant's voice faded and became indistinct as he went into the kitchen. Eleanor could hear her son's piping voice raised in protest and the deeper rumble of Grant, still berating him. She swung her feet over the side of the bed, intending to go and intervene. She swayed dizzily as she came upright, then sank back down on the bed.

No, she told herself. I have to let them have it out. I can't interfere, if I'm going to let Grant help me raise Phillip. If I interfere each time I think Grant's being too hard on him, we'll never have any peace. But how hard it is! she thought with anguish. Why can't Grant have a little more compassion, empathy? Why? Why? She lay back down on her pillows and pulled the blanket up high around her shoulders feeling dreadful as she listened to the muffled wrangling in the kitchen.

Presently Grant returned with a neatly laid tray bearing a bowl of soup, crisp fingers of melba toast and a tall, cool-looking glass of orange juice. There was a single spray of delicate looking baby's breath in a bud vase on one corner of the tray.

"Here you are," said Grant gently. "Sit up

straighter and hold onto the tray while I fix your pillows." He did so, keeping his face carefully averted from hers, she noticed, trying to feel amused, but managing to feel only an odd bitterness.

"This is lovely, Grant," she smiled, hoping to make up for nasty thoughts. "I don't have words to tell you how much I appreciate it."

"When you're better, you can show me. In fact, if it weren't for my job . . . care of the travelling public, you know . . . I'd make you show me right now! You look so kissable, Ellie, red nose and all."

"Oh, Grant, I know how you feel about germs, and I do understand."

"Germs, schmerms," he responded, bestowing a loving look upon her. "I've a good mind to say to heck with the customers, and kiss you anyway. It's not every day the girl of my dreams agrees to become my wife and after all, they're your germs. What's yours is mine!" But Eleanor noticed he made no attempt to kiss her, for all his brave words.

"Sort of . . . love me, love my germs?" she quipped, tasting the chicken soup he had brought. It tasted like warm water, and when Grant gave her a smile and a nod, she went on, touching on the subject she had been wondering how to approach with tact.

"Then don't you think you could try to love my son a little, Grant?"

"Oh, Ellie . . ." Grant sounded genuinely sorry. He rubbed a hand over his immaculate hair, mussing it, giving himself an oddly boyish look. "I just can't seem to get through to him!" he said worriedly. "He doesn't like me, you know, and that makes it doubly difficult for me to talk to him. I've never been good with kids, and knowing he hates me, resents me, makes it worse. The kid seems to get my back up every time he opens his mouth." Grant sighed, then went on hopefully. "But it will all work out. All the boy needs is a little firm discipline, as I've pointed out before. Take lunch time for example; I had a salami sandwich made for him, and then he decided he wanted peanut butter. He put up a bit of a battle, but when he saw I meant business, he ate the salami. Now he's gone outside to play."

"But Grant!" cried Eleanor indignantly. "You know he can't eat salami! Did you give him a choice, or did you just arbitrarily force the salami on him? Oh, darn you! You know it's too spicy for him!" This subject had come up once before, on a picnic for which Grant's cook had prepared the meal. Phillip had eaten the sliced meat, and become ill.

"The kid has to learn to do things he

doesn't like, and to eat things he doesn't like. Those are just simple facts of life, Ellie, and the sooner he learns it, the better it will be for all of us. Do you think I like making him, and therefore you, unhappy?"

Him, yes! The thought popped into Eleanor's mind before she could squelch it. She felt ashamed at once. Maybe not me, but I fully believe that you go out of your way to antagonise Phillip. Aloud she said, "Grant, I hate to say this, but the date of our wedding largely hinges upon Phillip's acceptance of the fact that you are to be his stepfather. I really think if you'd try a bit more tact and patience, you'd have him eating out of your hand just as you do your horses. Look how gentle and kind you are with me! And I'm a grown woman, accustomed to fighting my own battles. Why not see if you could try a little of the same treatment on a small boy who will be seeing his world, as he knows it, falling apart?"

"Now look here, Ellie," said Grant severely, standing up and glaring down at her. "Don't go using that kid as an excuse to put off our wedding day one moment longer than it legally must be! Think about this while I'm away: That boy of yours will be gone in another eleven or twelve years and then you'll be a sad, lonely woman if you allow him to rule your life now!"

He walked out, leaving her to her now-cold soup, for which she had no appetite anyway. Eleanor nibbled at a strip of toast, drank some of the juice and put the tray on the floor. She lay back, trying to think, but her fever-befuddled brain refused to co-operate.

When Grant returned in an hour, his mood seemed to have improved. "Hello, love," he greeted her from the doorway. Eleanor opened her eyes. "I have to go now, Ellie. I'm going back to Kamloops so I can get that all wound up and be back to you early the week after next. Get better, my darling, and try to have those proceedings well underway when I come home."

He picked up the tray, put the glass of juice on the bedside table and said, "The soup, I won't force on you. But you drink every drop of that orange juice. It's freshly squeezed . . . none of that frozen stuff for my girl when she's sick!"

"You are good to me," Eleanor said, smiling at him, trying to show without words that she was sorry for their argument. "I'm more grateful to you than I can say."

"I don't want your gratitude," he replied heavily. Then, with a change of tone, "I've made a casserole for you and . . . Phillip."

He seemed almost to choke on the boy's name. "It's in the oven, and all you'll have to do is turn it on at four. See you in a week and a half!"

He waved a cheerful hand at her and was gone.

Phillip forced down the salami sandwich, gagging at the greasy taste in his mouth, gulped his milk, scooped up his dog and dashed out of the house, without once looking at or speaking to the man who was making himself so much at home in his mother's kitchen. Some of the things Grant had said to him were still ringing in his unhappy mind. He ran until he was out of sight of the house then walked disconsolately toward the clearing. He had such a lot to think about and the salami was sitting heavily on his stomach.

He slumped into the clearing and caught sight of Jeff. His need for comfort became paramount and he ran to the man, flinging himself against Jeff's legs, ignoring the close proximity of the horse, the fact that he was loose, and bawled.

Jeff dropped to his knees and held the boy close until the howling stopped. "What's up, sport?"

"Grant came back and yelled at me to

shut up because my mom's sick and he made me put Casey outside and he made me eat a salami sandwich and now my tummy hurts!" Phillip's tummy, at that very moment, rebelled, and in short order hurt no more, but felt distinctly better, if somewhat empty.

"Come over to the creek and wash out your mouth, son, and I'll wipe off your face for you," said Jeff. He lifted the boy in his arms and cradled him tenderly as he carried him to the edge of the creek. There was a hard cast to his mouth, an oddly blazing fury in his eyes, but he was gentle as he cared for the little boy. To take Phillip's mind off his troubles for a few moments before he began questioning the child, as he knew he must, Jeff said, "Did you know that this creek runs into the Thompson, and the Thompson runs into the Fraser and together the two of them run bumping over rocks, around mountains, and through canyons until they get to the ocean? And did you know that the explorers used the river as roads when they first came here to learn about our country?"

Phillip nodded gravely. "My mom told me. She used to help me make boats and we'd float them down the creek so that they could go all the way to the ocean. We used to pretend that somewhere my father would find one, if he's still alive and he'd wonder if we had made it and sent it off to see him. She said there was gold in the creeks, too and people used to take it out in pans. But she didn't tell me about the explorers so I guess she didn't know that." The mention of his mother seemed to be upsetting, as tears flooded his eyes again. Jeff picked him up once more and carried Phillip to the shade at the side of the cabin.

When he had the child comfortable in the crook of his arm, sitting warm and secure in his lap, he said, "Now tell me what this is all about? Is your mom really sick?"

Phillip nodded tearfully and said, "She was in bed when I got home for lunch and Grant came out of her room and told me to shut up. Then he squeezed her some oranges for juice and made some soup and put it all on a tray . . . with a flower!" he added disgustedly. "He did the dishes and cleaned up the house and that's why Casey couldn't stay in and have lunch with me. My mom lets him and I told Grant but he said that my mom wasn't going to be boss much longer 'cause she was going to see a man after the weekend and when the judge said it's O.K., she's going to marry him and he'll be the boss!" Phillip gulped in air, buried his head against Jeff and wailed. "An' he said when they get married, real, real soon, we'll be leaving our house and going to live at the motel and Casey can't go 'cause dogs don't b'long at motels and I won't ever see you again and I won't see the log cabin and give Siwash apples!"

Jeff rocked the child in his arms, feeling a wash of deep and bitter anger. He held Phillip, letting him have his cry, then he said, "No more, my son. Don't cry any more. There, now . . . don't. Here, blow your nose and listen to me."

When Phillip was sitting quiet and attentive, his eyes raised with trust to Jeff's face, that man felt such a surge of fury, of futile hatred rush over him, that he clenched his fists until the knuckles showed white. Mixed in with that deep and bitter anger was a fear, a fear that what he was about to tell this child might never be. But Phillip needed help, and he needed it now! To hell with the letter of the law! Laws, if need be, could be broken, and surely no mother would deprive her son of . . . Phillip stirred restlessly.

"Sport, how'd you like it if I told you you could spend every summer with me in the cabin, even if your mother does marry Grant? Would that make you feel better about having him for a step-father?"

"I'd rather have you as a step-father," sniffed Phillip.

"Just not possible, Phil, but think about what I said, will you? You and me and Siwash and Casey, every summer, for your whole vacation, living here in the clearing. Sound good?"

Phillip nodded, and Jeff went on. "Then listen to me. Your mother loves you but she loves Grant, too, or she wouldn't want to marry him. And if you keep on fighting Grant every time you see him, you're going to make your mom very sad. Now, I know you're sad, too, Phil, and that's why I thought that if we made plans to live together every summer, for as many summers as you like, you might feel a little happier about having your mom love Grant, too."

"But she loves a ghost, remember? Did Grant mean my real father, Jeff, when he said she was in love with a ghost? How come big people have to love other big people?"

"I think maybe Grant did mean your real father, Phillip, but it would seem that your mom has decided she doesn't love him any more. And why should she? Didn't he go away a long, long time ago and never come back? Even if he had the best reasons in the world for not coming home, she couldn't have gone on loving him, waiting for him forever. We can't expect that of her, son."

"But we never had a dad in our house before, Jeff, so why do we have to have one now?" The tears welled up again in spite of Jeff's promise of summers together. The thought of the times when it was not summer were overwhelmingly larger than brief summer vacations.

"Phil, I can't explain that to you," answered Jeff sadly. "But it's true that you do have to have a dad in your house sooner or later. Your mom loves Grant and it's up to us, to you and me, to see that she gets a chance to be happy with him." Jeff pushed Phillip upright, saying, "Hey! Look at Si and Casey!" and laughing.

Phillip looked over at the dog and horse. The puppy was cavorting around the horse's feet and Siwash had his nose down, snuffling at the noisy little pup. The big nose would bump the puppy, who would fall, roll over and come right back for more. Phillip giggled, tears forgotten for the moment, and ran in between the horse's feet to get Casey.

"Bad boy!" he scolded. "You're not supposed to bite Si's nose!" As Jeff watched, silent, tense and alert, holding his breath, Phillip reached up and patted the horse's nose. "Poor old Si," he said sympathetically, "I won't let him do it again."

Jeff limped over and unhooked Siwash's bridle from the limb where it hung. "Would you take Si back to his stall, Phillip, please? He knows he's not supposed to be out when you're here."

"Oh!" For the first time Phillip realised that the horse was loose and that he had patted the big beast, even walked by those enormous feet to take the puppy away! "Jeff!" he cried, "Jeff! I'm not scared of him! Look!" And he stepped closer once more, reaching up his hand to stroke Siwash's neck, patting him, telling the horse he was sorry about all the time Si had spent locked up like a prisoner.

Jeff lifted the puppy from Phillip's arms and set it on the back of the horse. "Let's give Casey a ride," he suggested easily, as if puppies rode horse-back every day of the week.

"Oh, no! He'll fall off!" Phillip cried in a panic.

"Then maybe you should sit up there with him and hold him on," said Jeff quietly, off-handedly. It didn't matter a bit to him whether or not Phillip deprived Casey of the pleasure of a ride. "Do you want a saddle, or would you rather go bare-back like the Indian braves did?"

Phillip shook, but he raised his head to look with steady eyes at Jeff's quiet, relaxed face, then back at the puppy, still held in position by Jeff's big hand. Casey looked awfully small 'way up there, and awfully alone, too, but he didn't look one bit scared! He was grinning his puppy-kind of grin, wagging his long brush of a tail. "I'll go bareback," he said firmly.

Jeff lifted him up and kept steadying hands tight around his waist. "Lean forward," he instructed calmly, "and hold Casey between your elbows. Put your fingers deep into Si's mane. Go on, hold tight. You won't hurt him. And pull your knees up, squeeze them against Si's sides. O.K.?"

Tremulously, Phillip said, "O-O.K. . . ."

"Good!" cheerfully. "You look great. Now let's take Casey for a little walk around the clearing." Jeff led the horse out at a slow and steady pace with Phillip clinging to the mane until his knuckles turned white. Once, twice, three times around the clearing they went, and the horse, seemingly aware of the importance of his mission, stepped with care over and around each obstacle on the rough ground.

"O.K., that's all," said Jeff, leading Siwash to his stable. "Come on, give me

Casey, then you get down by putting your foot on the top of the door." He took the pup and set him on the ground. "Or," he added casually, "do you want to go around once more by yourself?"

"Wi-without you holding the reins?" Phillip's eyes were round and frightened. "I think I'll get down now." He climbed to the top of the lower section of the Dutch door and dropped to the ground.

"That's the way," smiled Jeff. "Put Siwash in his stall, please, Phil." Without waiting to see that Phillip complied with his request, he walked off toward the cabin, the puppy romping at his heels.

A few minutes later when a triumphant Phillip joined Jeff at the side of the cabin, he looked up to see that the roof was nearly completed. "Can we finish it up now?" he begged.

They worked for an hour and when the last shake had been firmly nailed to the ridge pole Jeff said, "How about something to replace that lunch you lost?"

Once more during the afternoon Jeff got the boy on the back of the horse, and once more Phil rejected the idea that he should try to take the horse alone. "Maybe tomorrow," he said. "Today I don't want to."

But Sunday was the same. He made many

circuits of the clearing with Jeff leading Siwash and even began to sit straighter. Late Sunday afternoon Jeff said, "That's it for today, son. I'm going to Vancouver and I won't be here all day tomorrow. Think you could come and give Si his oats?"

"Sure. How come you have to go away, Jeff?"

"I have to see a man, son. It's important, or I wouldn't leave, but I should be back late in the evening after you're in bed. I'll see you on Tuesday after school, right?"

"Right."

"How's your mom, really? You didn't say when I asked you this morning."

"She says she's all right, but she was lying down on the couch when I got home for lunch and she let me make my own sandwich. I had honey and Casey had dog food. Mom sure can cough, Jeff! She coughs better than anybody! She sounds like the dogs the game warden brought in to hunt down a cougar last winter." Phillip was definitely impressed by his mother's ability to imitate the hounds. Jeff, however, was not.

"Are Kathy and Bill on the farm?" he asked, frowning.

"Yup. They don't go out much now. Kathy says because they're waiting for their baby. I guess they have to stay home the same way my mom does if she's waiting for a C.O.D. parcel." Phillip gave Jeff a conspiratorial look. "I hope her cough is still bad tomorrow so she can't go and tell the judge to say my father's dead. Won't that make Grant mad?"

Jeff made his face look stern. "I thought we agreed that if we could, we'd help your mom to be happy by treating Grant a little nicer? So we can have summers together?"

"Oh . . . yes. I forgot. I hope she feels a little better tomorrow. See you, Jeff."

On Monday morning Eleanor staggered around, got her son off to school before she crawled back into her bed. There she remained until the hammering on her door brought her out of a restless and feverish sleep. It was Bill.

"Kathy . . ." he panted. "The baby . . . babies . . ."

"Oh, Bill," said Eleanor through her nose, "that's great!" She tried to inject enthusiasm into her voice. "Thanks for letting me know. Come back and tell me when it's all over." She swayed, caught the door frame and forced a smile.

Bill was too excited to notice that she was really unwell. He knew she was suffering from a cold, but that was all. "I've been in touch with Ralph Exley and he'll send a man over to supervise the milking and all the rest of it; the boys will just put in their normal hours, so you'll be alone here for the night. I wish you'd get a phone down here! But anyway, here's the keys, and call on Ralph if you need anything."

"Fine, Bill. Now scoot back to Kathy and drive carefully. The stork's never in a furious rush for first babies."

Bill took off at a gallop up the hill and as she climbed shivering back into her bed, Eleanor heard the gravel spray against the stone wall near the end of the driveway. Bill, ignoring her admonition, was driving like a maniac . . . or a man whose wife was about to give birth.

How wonderful it must be to have an anxious husband drive you to the hospital when your child is about to be born, she thought, and wiping a tear of self pity from her face, she huddled deeper into her bed. All I had was an old father, hovering hopefully, praying that I'd give him a grandson to take over the farm.

Phillip came home some time after that and Eleanor called out to him that he could have a couple of cookies, some milk or juice. "Don't forget to feed Casey before you go out to play," she told him, adding that she would get up and fix his supper at half-past five, so be on time.

Phillip did as he was told, quietly for once, and she heard the screen door shut, heard his feet pounding along the path as he headed for the creek and ultimately, the woods.

Eleanor dozed, woke and reached for her glass of water. It fell over as she tried to pick it up and she was aware of the sound of water trickling onto the floor. She struggled to sit up, to reach for something with which to mop up and the trickling of water became a hollow, rushing roar which thundered in her ears, flooded over her, black and deep, washing her away, taking her off into some other, far place, drowning . . . black . . . deep . . .

Phillip came home after feeding Siwash and tried to wake his mother. She moaned a little but wouldn't talk to him. Shrugging, he wandered into the kitchen, not yet worried, just a little peeved that she should be so sleepy when he was so hungry.

He fed Casey half a can of dog food, even though he had given him bread and milk not two hours before, and when he was looking in the fridge for that, he found some of the casserole Grant had made on Saturday. It didn't taste very good cold, but Phillip didn't quite know how to make it warm, so he ate it anyway. He finished off his meal with a few peaches out of a bottle Kathy had sent down a couple of days before.

After he ate, Phillip played with Casey, but the silence from his mother's room disturbed him. Holding the puppy in his arms he went and sat on the end of her bed and watched her sleep. She sure was rolling around a lot, he thought, and making funny noises. He tried again to wake her up and make her talk to him and when she wouldn't, he decided he'd go and talk to Kathy and Bill. Maybe Mommy would wake up for them.

Kathy and Bill were gone away. The two big boys who helped Bill, Curtis and Mike, had gone home. The cows were all there, the milking had been done. There was fresh fodder in the feed bins. Bill had finished all his chores before he went out. Maybe they wouldn't be back until late, so he'd better go home and see if Mommy . . . no! that was for babies! . . . see if Mom would talk to him now. He didn't like the farm to be so quiet, to see Bill's car gone and no lights in the big house. It was like there was no one home but him and Casey.

As he opened the screen door Phillip

could hear his own heart thundering in his ears and he smashed the door shut, just to hear the noise it made. It made the silence deeper. He turned on the TV and the sound of rifle fire ricocheting through sandstone hills was too loud. He turned it off and watched the pin-point of light die out in the centre of the screen, then looked out the windows.

It was getting dark and he was tired. Maybe if he went to bed all by himself like a big boy Mommy . . . Mom would be better in the morning and would talk to him.

Phillip took a slice of bread, clumsily spread it with peanut butter and poured himself a glass of milk. He put Casey in his basket on the back porch, idly watched two tiny black ants swimming in the peach juice he had dripped on the table at supper time then, munching his bread, he went to look at his mother again.

Her face was all funny looking. It seemed little somehow, and white. She made an odd noise in her throat and was still rolling around in her bed. Phillip stared hard at her, put his glass on her dresser and went across the hall into his own room.

Much later he awoke to find it very, very dark and a noise which scared him and made him want to cry was coming from somewhere. He jumped out of his bed, crying, "Mommy! Mommy!" and ran across the hall to her room. "Mom, there's a bad noi . . ." He stopped. The bad noise was coming from his mother's bed . . . she was making it! He went to her, touched her and jumped back. She sure did feel hot, and that noise she was making hurt his head, made his ears ring, sort of like Casey when he thought he wasn't going to get fed, only this went on and on!

"Mom, do you want a drink of water?" She said this to him sometimes at night. No answer, only the noise. "Mommy, do you want me to get Bill and Kathy?" And suddenly his seven year old mind told him he'd better not hang around here asking questions, waiting for answers which would not be given: He'd better get Kathy and Bill or someone! And fast!

Bill's car was still not back. Jeff! Phillip decided. I'll get Jeff! He'll know what to do!

The small pyjama-clad figure dashed off across the meadow and disappeared into the forest, knowing by instinct the dark path which cut between the trees and into the clearing. He streaked across the opening in the forest, past the cabin and as he neared the lean-to, Siwash whinnied gently, snorting in the night. Phillip started, froze for an instant, then remembered that the horse was his friend. He carried on to the place where the camper was always parked.

It was gone!

And then Phillip remembered. Jeff wouldn't be back until late. But wasn't it late now? It was dark! And his mom was sick and he had to get a big person to help! He sobbed once, thinking of the long walk down the highway to Mr. Exley's house . . . then, he recalled the snorting whinny of Siwash . . .

As the little boy led the big horse out of the darkness of the path, the moon came sailing up from behind the mountain, lighting the forestry road and making the shadows blacker. Phillip shivered as much with fear as with cold, but he led the horse to a point near a large stump, and talking to Siwash the way he had heard Jeff do, he climbed from the stump onto the horse's back. His fingers clung to Siwash's mane and knees clung to the warm flanks. He leaned forward and said, "Go, boy!" but the horse stood still. Oh, how did Jeff make him go? Then the reins hanging down where he had left them after leading Si here caught his eye.

The child struggled to reach the leather strap and finally managed to capture it without dismounting. He caught the reins tightly in his small paws and as he pulled up on them the horse raised his head and slowly walked forward down the forestry road toward the highway.

Phillip was nearly at the turn-off and wondering desperately what he would do to make Si go in the right direction when they got there, when the twin beams of headlights swept across him, blindingly. Siwash stepped carefully to the edge of the track as the camper screeched to a stop, its rear end slewing in the loose dirt.

"Phillip!" cried Jeff. "What are you doing?"

"Mommy . . . my mom's making funny noises, she's sick and she's making noises! Bill and Kathy's are gone away and you were gone too so me and Si was going to get Mr. and Mrs. Exley!" Phillip was shivering, his teeth were chattering, but Jeff could make sense out of what the child said. Before the last word was out of the trembling lips, the truck had been shut down, lights off and Jeff was swinging up behind Phillip on the back of the horse. His jacket was wrapped around the boy and the horse was turned.

"All right, son. I'll take care of your mom for you. That was a brave thing you did, sport, riding Siwash all by yourself when you've never done it before."

Phillip felt the tempo of hoof-beats quicken under him as Jeff urged Siwash out of a trot and into a gallop. He felt warm, suddenly, no longer afraid, and the horse was carrying him . . . cathumpity, cathumpity . . . along with Jeff . . . cathumpity, cathumpity . . . back to his mother. He felt like laughing! Riding fast was fun! "Hey, Jeff! Aren't you going to call the Sheriff 'cause I rustled your horse?"

Jeff made a deep sound in his chest. "No!" he called back over the noise of the horse. Phillip didn't know the word jubilation, but he recognised the sound of it in Jeff's voice. "I'm proud of you, my son!"

When they arrived in the yard in front of the cottage Jeff flung himself off the horse, and with Phillip tucked under his arm, he ran to the house. He dumped Phillip in his bed, bundled the blankets tight around him for warmth and bent to kiss the forehead of the little boy. "I'm going to look after your mom, Phil. When you're warm again, you can come in and see her."

Phillip smiled sleepily in the dark. "I knew you'd come and help, Jeff," he said, but he got no answer beyond the sound of Jeff's voice across the hall. He wondered for a minute why Jeff was saying that, but he was too warm and sleepy and contented to wonder long. It seemed right, somehow for Jeff to be saying, "Eleanor! Eleanor! Sweetheart, for God's sake tell me what's wrong! Oh, sweet lady . . ."

SEVEN

As David's hands touched Eleanor, his lost, beloved wife, he could feel the terrible heat burning under her skin which was dry and taut. She was moaning, tossing restlessly, saying incomprehensible things between clenched teeth.

"All right, Eleanor," he said in his most gentle voice, a voice which he thought with a tinge of amazement sounded as if it should not be working at all. "All right, my sweet, I'm here and I'm going to help you. Lie still, my darling. I have to leave you for a minute or two, but I'll come back to you." Was he getting through to her at all? She seemed less agitated, the moaning was quieter, wasn't it? The wild thrashing had diminished, if nothing else! He placed his cool hands around her face tenderly, kissed her burning forehead and loped from the room.

Into the living room he dashed, glanced around rapidly, then ran for the kitchen, his eyes seeking, raking the hall as he crossed it, and still he couldn't find it, not even in the kitchen! Where was the phone? Dammit!

He needed a phone! He needed a doctor for Eleanor, and he needed one now!

There was no phone! What do I do now? he asked himself, standing still, trying to collect his thoughts. I don't dare leave her to find help, and that fever has got to be brought down! The fever, that's the big thing right now! Whatever else ails her, if I can just get that fever down, half the battle will be won. Think, man; Think! Remember!

He bolted for the bathroom, unerringly, and wrenched open the medicine cabinet. Rubbing alcohol. The memory of the sweet-faced nun who had cared for him was in the front of his mind, now. It was her hands which guided his, her voice which spoke to him calmly as he found a basin, mixed alcohol with water, put a cloth in it, took a large towel from the linen closet and filled a hot-water bottle. Ice. He remembered ice at the back of his neck, the hot bottle at his feet.

He wrapped ice from the freezer in a towel and plastic and returned, laden, to Eleanor.

She was thrashing wildly once more, calling, "David . . . David . . . you were here and you went away . . . Dave . . ." So his voice had broken through the wall of fever!

His presence had been what had calmed her!

"Hush, darling. Hush. I'm here. Sit up." Gentle hands lifted her, slid the nightgown off her, straightened the sheet under her, making it feel cool and even. The ice pack was lumpy under her neck, but so lovely and cold, and there was heat, too much heat next to her burning feet. "No, darling, leave it there. It's to keep you from getting chilled."

He draped the large towel over her, as the nun had done for him when she refused to let him die, and began to bathe Eleanor. First her face, and then her arms and hands, one at a time, not drying them, letting the alcohol evaporate to cool the awful fever from her skin. When one hand and arm were done, he returned to her face, then the next hand and arm, then the face, then the legs and feet, and in this manner, talking soothingly all the while, he worked over her.

Face, arms, face, legs, face, torso, and back to her face again, wetting her hair, praying deep inside and feeling terror at the rate with which the cloth became hot, at the rate with which the water in the basin took on the heat of her skin. Aspirin, he told himself. She must have aspirin! He dared to leave her, must dare to leave her and return to the bathroom! More cold water . . . more alcohol . . . and aspirin. Water in a glass . . . back to the bedroom.

"Sit up, sweet," he crooned, holding her against his chest. "Open your mouth. I'm going to put a pill on your tongue, give you water, and I want you to swallow. Do it for me, darling!"

Something in Eleanor was dimly aware of the orders being given her by this hallucination, and because she felt too weak to think about it, she simply accepted the fact that someone was here, someone was looking after her and she thought it was David. Of course it couldn't be, but whoever it was, she was being cared for, and she wasn't going to die and have Phillip find her in the morning. She was dimly grateful and opened her mouth when told, swallowed when told and repeated the process until three pills had been administered.

The bathing went on and on until she felt cold and shivery. Then a sheet was placed over her so lightly that she hardly knew it was there, and the voice said, "Sleep now, darling. I won't leave you." The phantom with cool, tender hands stroked the hair away from her face, and she managed to whisper, "Phillip . . . ?"

"He's all right. He's in bed."

Eleanor tried to smile him away, tried to tell him he didn't exist, but he made her feel so much better, hallucination or not, that she decided to let him stay. "Stay . . . David . . . stay . . . let me . . . pretend . . . little longer . . ."

And the phantom's voice went with her into sleep. "I'll stay forever, Eleanor."

David Jefferson sat in a big chair, one he had sat in long before, and watched his sleeping wife as he had also done long before. Then, with a tender smile on his face, he tiptoed across the hall and looked down on the face of his sleeping son, a thing he had never done before . . .

"My son," he whispered softly. "My son . . . and my wife. My home . . ." He looked around the darkened cottage. Are they mine? he cried inside, are they? Or will I have to leave them again? Oh, no! Never! After all this time, all the years during which they have been dead to me, to return and find them alive, it would be too much for the fates to expect me to leave. She loves me, does my warm and living Eleanor who is not dead!

He went back to her then and sat in the big chair by her side, looking down on her, drinking in the sight of her, knowing she belonged to him and would never marry that other man! She loved him . . . David . . . not Grant! It had been him she had called for, him, and him alone for whom she had waited with faith and loyalty all these long years!

I should have checked, he berated himself for the thousandth time in the past few months. Why, oh why did I leave it so long before coming back? He knew that answer: There had been nothing . . . no one to come back to . . .

Eleanor stirred. With her eyes squeezed tightly shut, her face tense, she huddled under the one sheet he had covered her with. "What is it, darling? Are you too hot again?" His hand touched her face.

She shook the bed with her shivering. "Cold," she muttered. "So cold . . . make me warm . . . I'm c-cold!" He piled blankets on her. Still she shook. Her teeth rattled in her head, and he knew, he remembered, that her muscles would be aching with the force of the spasms shaking her body . . . it had been that way with him, and he did what the nun had been unable to do for him, he did it for his wife . . .

For not one split second did he hesitate, this was his wife! She was cold and she needed him! David stripped to the skin and slid his warm body into the bed beside his shivering wife. His long, naked warmth touched her icy flesh and she snuggled close into the curve of his body, coming into his arms as naturally as if she had been there yesterday. He drew in one long, anguished breath and held her against his chest, his arms wrapping around her back tightly, crossing over, his hands rubbing her arms, stroking, warming, comforting . . .

Eleanor sighed, deeply contented. "David . . . your boniness . . . gone." Then, presently, as the shivering subsided, she nestled closer, malleable and silken, moulding herself to him, every inch touching, bringing him the most exquisite pleasure and pain . . .

"Mos' substantial h'lucination . . ." she muttered.

"Lie still, sweet lady," rumbled a deeply resonant voice in the ear which was pressed to the warm chest. "Lie still, and we'll sleep . . . just so. Are you warm?"

"So warm, my darling, my David, so lovely and warm . . ."

David was up long before the clock in the kitchen showed half-past seven. At that time he went to Eleanor, checked. She was still sleeping, still had that same look of wonder on her face. He touched her gently

. . . she was damp, a fine film of moisture beaded her upper lip. He put another blanket on her and went to wake his son.

Shaking the boy by the shoulder, he said, "Wake up sport! What do you want for breakfast . . . porridge, or eggs?"

The child opened his eyes, startled at first, then he beamed. "Jeff!" he said gladly. "What are you do . . ." Before he could complete his question, he remembered. "Mommy . . . ? My mom?"

"She's much better, Phil. Sleeping, but lots and lots better. She's not making that noise any more." He knew it had been the noise which had worried Phillip most. "Tell you what, let me know what you want to eat, and while I get it started, you peek in the door and look at your mother. But don't you dare wake her!"

Phillip scampered from his bed and darted to his mother's door. Before he opened it, he turned and whispered hoarsely, "C'n you really make porridge . . . with raisins in it?"

Jeff nodded solemnly. "I can. And with brown sugar on it?"

Phillip nodded back, grinning from ear to ear, his grey eyes alight with joy as he slowly pushed open his mother's door.

A happy little boy quickly dressed, pretended to wash his face and ran to the back porch to feed his dog. The horse, whom until that moment had been completely forgotten by man and boy alike, was eating his way around the rose arbour, nibbling the tender new shoots, sneezing at the pollen in the small, golden blossoms.

"Hey! Si! Quit eatin' my mom's roses!" yelled Phillip, running out into the yard and dragging at the reins which were hanging down in front of the horse.

Jeff appeared in the doorway, bare-foot shirtless and wearing a frilly apron over his trousers. Phillip giggled. "Keep it down, sport," Jeff admonished quietly. "Mom's sleeping, remember? Come on, now. Let's snap it up or you'll be late for the school bus!"

"But I gotta stay home and look after my mom!" Phillip's lower lip jutted out ominously, trembling.

"Oh, no you don't," smiled the man. "That's what you have me for. It's my privilege, son!" He threw the boy over his shoulder and galloped into the house where he dumped Phillip on a chair. "Just like a sack of potatoes," he said. "Now eat up all that porridge."

Phillip ate, drank a glass of apple juice and grabbed up his lunch kit. It was empty!

"Jeff! I can't go to school! You haven't made my lunch!"

"Oh, I'm a lousy mother, aren't I?" asked Jeff, quickly throwing together a bologna sandwich, wrapping up cookies and dumping an orange in beside them. "Milk in the thermos?" he asked, and not waiting for an answer, he filled the bottle, slipped it into its slot and clamped the lid of the lunch kit closed. "Here, take it and run!" he said. "The bus will be here in two minutes!"

Phillip stared in amazement. "How d'you know what time my bus comes?"

"I know lots of things, now quit stalling and take off or I'll chase you all the way there!" He made a mock-threatening move toward Phillip, snapping a tea-towel at him. The child ran off down the lane, laughing.

David went back to his sleeping wife. He stood looking at her for a few moments before he silently and quickly slipped out of his clothes again. He lay beside her, not touching her, and pulled the covers up around them both, needing only to be close to her. After a time, being close was not enough. He ran a gentle fingertip down her spine, wondering if that, too, would be the same.

It was! She moaned softly, and turned, as he had hoped she would, still sleeping into

151

his arms. This, he thought, is heaven! He closed his eyes and let the sweet sensations of her softness, her nearness, flood over him. He let one finger stroke the hair on her temple, afraid to move, afraid to wake her, but needing to caress her. She slept on, her soft cheek resting against his chest, her head fitting into the hollow beneath his chin, fitting as it always had and she tightened her arms around him, whispering, ". . . love you . . ."

"I love you too, my own sweet lady," he replied softly, hoping she would know in her dreams that it was true.

In her dreams she heard, and half in a dream she felt the warm breath on her cheek, felt the gentle finger-tip on her temple, and knew she was dreaming a sweet dream of David, a phantom David who had come to her when she lay ill, who had made her cool when she was too hot, and then made her gently warm when she was freezing, and the half dream left her, leaving reality behind, but the reality was as the dream had been.

Eleanor opened her eyes. She saw a brown shoulder in the immediate foreground. It was curved up and around her, blocking her view of all else, and she shut her eyes tightly for a moment, coming fully awake, fully aware of the protectiveness inherent in the curvature of that shoulder as it shielded her. Protectiveness and possessiveness, too, were in the arms which held her and Eleanor gasped slightly, opening her eyes again.

At once she was released from the warmth of the embrace which had held her while she slept. She lay back on her pillow while the man beside her rose up on the elbow and looked down at her with David's grey eyes, and smiled David's dear smile surrounded by a thick beard. He spoke in David's well-remembered voice . . .

"Good morning, sweet lady."

She could feel him touching her, feel his warm length along the flesh of her body, and tears filled her eyes. She could not speak, for all the things she needed to say, needed to ask were making such a tangled mess in her brain. The tears overflowed and trickled down into her ears. She ignored them and looked up at him through a mist, her face working, her throat thick, unable to move. With vast effort, she managed to speak at last. Eleanor opened her trembling mouth and said, "The roses did grow."

At that, David buried his face against her breast and together they wept for years lost, for joy regained, and for happiness yet to come. Her hands went up from his back to tangle in his dark hair and she pulled his face up to hers, her mouth asking for his kisses which were given and returned, and more . . . so much, much more . . .

Later, he smiled down at her and said huskily, "You can tell Grant for me that you are most definitely not frigid!"

At David's mention of Grant, her world, the present, and all the people in it came rushing back upon her. "Phillip!" she gasped. "He's got to go to school!"

"He's gone," said David, pulling her back into his arms. "He had porridge . . . with raisins in and brown sugar on . . . fed the dog, chased the horse out of our roses and even remembered to tell me to make his lunch. He tried to stall, so he could miss the bus, but I rousted him out in a hurry."

"You . . . rousted him out? What horse? You gave him breakfast . . . made his lunch? But how . . . how long have you been here? How long was I sick? What's going on?"

"One at a time, sweet," he laughed at her, holding her tightly. "No. Stay still," as she tried to pull away from him. "Come back to me, darling!"

Eleanor jumped out of the bed, out of reach of those seeking hands, and stood there, trembling, wide-eyed. She grabbed her robe and wrapped it around herself, suddenly conscious of her nudity. "Get out!" she croaked. "Let me get dressed! What are you thinking of, coming back into my life like this without warning, catching me when I'm too sick to think, to fight back? Oh, God!" she cried, and sank into the chair. "Oh, God! What have I done? I promised to marry Grant! David! You here! I can't take it in! You'll have to go! Leave me! Let me think!"

"I can't, sweetheart. I don't have any clothes on. You're sitting on my pants."

"I'm . . . ?" Wildly she jumped up, threw his trousers at him and fled from the room.

She was still terribly weak and feeling quite miserable, she realised as she huddled in a dejected little heap on the couch in the living room. David . . . David! Here! It was too much to believe! How could it be? Where in God's name had he been? And how, how in the world had he known about Grant's calling her frigid?

He filled the doorway, shirtless, barefoot, hair standing on end, and looked at her with grave, concerned eyes.

"How . . . ? I mean . . . why? You aren't the same shape!" she cried accusingly, her mouth, bruised from his kisses, a-tremble.

"No, darling. When you last saw me I was

twenty-four. A man fills out in that many years, Eleanor." He limped over and sat beside her heavily, not touching, but looking, looking . . .

"You limp," she said more quietly, but with the same accusing note in her tone.

He nodded. "My leg was injured when I got lost. Before I was found it had become quite badly infected. Part of the thigh muscle was destroyed."

"You . . . you knew about Grant's calling me frigid . . ." she stammered. "How?"

"Phillip."

"Phillip? But he . . . how?" She shook her head in bewilderment.

"He asked me if it were a bad word." David reached out a hand and gently stroked the hair out of her eyes. "He said it made you mad and you didn't even say good-night to Grant." She jerked away from his touch, and he said, "I want some coffee, Eleanor. You?"

"Coffee! You come waltzing in here like you belong and want coffee? Offer it to me in my own home, before you even tell me how you came to be here?"

"Your home? Who built it, sweet lady?" She glared at him, speechless. "You always were bad-tempered before you had your morning coffee, weren't you?" He ducked, grinning, out of the room and the cushion she threw at him, missed.

David returned to the living room in a short while, a tray of coffee and tantalisingly aromaed cinnamon toast held carefully in front of him. He put it on the coffee table before her and said, "Sweet lady, you still make damn good cookies and doughnuts. Thanks for sending them over with Phil."

"Over . . . ?" she whispered, her eyes full of pain and bewilderment.

"To the log cabin!" impatiently. Then, "Now look, Eleanor! He told me he'd told you about me, about the cabin! That's the only reason I let him stay around for such long periods at a time. He said you weren't worried! He said he'd told you all about his friend Jeff, and I must say I wondered about your letting him be with a stranger!"

"Then . . . you . . . you're Jeff?" She wanted to laugh. She wanted to cry. "I thought you . . . Jeff, was an imaginary friend. He has them, you know! Solomon the Soldier, and we had to call him just that . . . Solomon wouldn't . . ." and she choked on her toast, put her cup down and wept wildly as David gathered her into his arms.

"You could have been anybody! A hobo, a drug addict, an escaped convict! I asked him once if he had seen any strangers around, anyone who didn't belong and he told me there was no one! And I didn't believe he had anybody there and the day I was feeling so terrible and Grant found me crying it was because Phillip had told me the cabin was right beside the dogwood tree! My God! To think there was really someone there with him all that time and I . . ."

"But it wasn't just 'someone', darling! It wasn't any of those terrible things you're thinking. It was me! And the first day I saw him he was just a little boy with a big load of problems, taking them out on a log with my axe because he couldn't use it on Grant."

"What do you mean?" Eleanor raised tear-drenched eyes to David. He kissed her nose gently and pushed her away.

"Drink your coffee, Eleanor."

"No! I want to know what you meant!"

"He was upset at something Grant had done to him. I was resting in the shade when I heard someone chopping with my axe. I took it away from him, and he disappeared, but he hung around in the trees watching me work, not knowing I knew he was there. I told a squirrel I needed help, because I felt sorry for the little guy. The next day when I went back to the glade the brush had been piled up and he was hovering in the trees again. You called him and he took off.

"Then, as the days went by, we became friends because we each needed a friend. Even before I knew who he was, what he was to me, I had learned that his mother was going to marry a man named Grant. So knowing that, how could I come to you, Eleanor? I had to wait, to see what was happening. If you had found someone else you truly loved, I was going to leave, let you have me declared legally dead, or let you divorce me for desertion if necessary. But," he added grimly, "not now! Now I have you, and I have my son, and I have a firm commitment to him. Regardless of what happens between you and me, Phillip and I are going to finish that cabin, and we are going to live in it together each and every summer holiday for as long as he wants! And you, and Grant, and all the courts in the land won't stop me from keeping that promise to my son!"

She stared at him and his grim face. "But why didn't you come to me as soon as you got back? Why did you start building a cabin on the Anderson place instead of coming to me? And why the Anderson place at all? It's private property, even if we did always treat that stretch of woods as our own! Why build in the little glade?"

David ignored the first two questions.

"The Anderson place is mine, Eleanor. I bought it. The glade was a wonderful part of my memories of you and I had to live there, to bring you close. If I couldn't have you, at least I could have that."

"Oh, David," she cried, reaching for him, holding him, being held by him. "It was so wonderful, our little glade, wasn't it?"

He did not answer her with words for a long time, and then, running a finger down her shoulder and arm, he said, "It will be again, sweet, so get well and we'll go back there together." He rebuttoned her robe to keep the draft from her precious skin and sat her up into the crook of his arm.

"It's just lucky for me that you weren't wearing this awful thing that night I watched you sit at your typewriter and not work, Eleanor Bear!"

"How did you know about Eleanor Bear?" she gasped.

"I know everything," he grinned, rubbing his beard against her face, "thanks to our talkative young Phillip."

"Did . . . did he volunteer all this information, or did you . . . ?"

"Pump him? I most certainly did," replied David, giving the one answer she had wanted to hear. "I found out you were not fat, that you didn't eat enough and Grant said it was because you were love-lorna — he thought that meant you were in love with Lorna, like he is — and that your hair is the colour of rootbeer popsicles."

Eleanor thumped him on the top of the head with a balled up fist. "Thanks a lot!" she laughed, and then sobered. "But that night . . . I knew someone was staring at me. I felt it. That's why I closed the drapes. And the next morning I saw your tracks by the rose arbour and was glad I had felt it necessary to lock the doors for once."

"A good thing, too," he said severely. "I might have been anybody . . . a hobo, a drug addict, an escaped convict!"

"Don't make fun of me! Why didn't you come to me that night? I dreamed of you, Dave; I used to dream about you a lot, but all that came through clearly even in the dreams was your voice. That night, though, I dreamed of your eyes. I wonder if my heart knew you were near?"

"It should have. You looked right into my eyes in the dining room at the motel. I knew the risk I was taking but I had to see you again! I had to see you with Phillip, and with that Grant person! I hoped the beard was enough to disguise my face in case you did happen to look at me. If it hadn't been for that little scamp grinning at me all evening, you never would have cast your eyes in my direction. Oh, darling! I wanted so badly to rush over and bust Grant right in the mouth! I wanted to drag you away from his table and bring you home and make passionate love to you! I didn't even sleep that night, so you were luckier than I; at least you had dreams!"

At that moment a loud knocking was heard on the door and Eleanor jumped to her feet. "Dave! Get up! Go into the bedroom!"

"Why, sweet? We're married."

Eleanor wrung her hands in agitation. "Go! Just go, please! I'm not ready yet to . . . to . . ."

"Share me?" he grinned. "Well get rid of whoever it is, and quick!" He ducked into the bedroom and shut the door. Eleanor shoved the extra plate and cup under the couch and went to the door.

It was Bill.

"Three!" he said, by way of greeting. "Three!"

"Three?" repeated Eleanor stupidly, then, as the light dawned, she squealed, "Triplets? Good grief! Three babies? Oh, Bill! How's Kathy?"

He beamed, jammed a cigar into her hand, and saying, "Oh, you won't want that," tried to snatch it back. Eleanor re-tained it, and he ran on, "Two boys and a girl! Kathy's tired but feeling great! We're naming them Graham, Steven and Eleanor, the boys for the two grandpas and the girl for our landlady! Oh, you are the landlady, aren't you? Hey, how's your cold? Kath said I was to ask. She thinks you're sicker than you know. Are you?"

Eleanor laughed weakly, said, "I'm all right," and spoiled it by coughing deeply in her chest. "Do you want to come in, Bill, or are you going right back?"

"I'm going back. I just came home for a change of clothes and to check up on the stock. See you, Ellie!" With that Bill was off, exuding excitement and joy.

Eleanor leaned dizzily against the table for a moment before she found the strength to go back to her bedroom. I surely am weak, she thought with a little giggle, and not just from the fever, either. She staggered light-headedly through the door of the bed-room, looking for David. He was gone!

"Dave?" she called, hearing the panic in her voice, trying to still it. "David?"

The silence in the house pressed into her ears, making them roar and she flung herself on the bed, still rumpled from the night before, and sobbed hysterically. "Did I dream you . . . David . . . David . . ." Then, "Oh! David! Don't you ever disappear like that again!" as he leapt out from under the bed and landed beside her wrapping her in his arms.

"Sorry, darling," he said, sounding contrite. "I shouldn't have teased you. You are sick, and your fever's coming back. I just wanted to see if you really wanted me back," he whispered against her mouth.

"Can you have any doubts?"

"Still a few, sweet lady of mine. Take them all away!"

"God!" she said. "How well I remember that lustful look of yours!"

"You aren't exactly the picture of an innocent, blushing bride, either, my sweet. Nor," he added teasingly, "do you act like a frigid woman."

"I'm not!" she cried gladly, "Oh, darling, I'm not, am I?"

They awoke an hour before Phillip was due home. David put his cool lips to Eleanor's brow. "Fever, darling," he said. "You stay here while I run a cool tub for you." He got out of bed and she watched sleepily as he went into the bathroom; dozed as the water thundered into the tub. He came back, lifted her and carried her into the bath. David sponged her quickly, dried her gently, fed her aspirins and slipped her into a clean, fresh nightgown. He left her wrapped in a blanket on the chair while he changed the linen on the bed and then helped her back into it.

"There you are, my lovely, sick darling. How many times I've lain awake nights thinking about this bed." He put his head down on her shoulder and Eleanor caressed his hair, loving the crisp feel of it between her fingers.

"Darling, go have a shower. Phillip will be home soon." Oh, how wonderful it was to make sounds like a wife! She lay there, thinking of all the wifely things she would be able to say to him now.

When he came back, she asked, "David, what do we tell Phillip?"

"The truth," he replied, rubbing his leg with the end of a towel.

"What . . ." What is the truth? she had been about to ask when she saw the scar on his thigh. It was long, wide and knotted, an angry purple pearled with white knobs, and sunken deep in his flesh. "Oh, darling!" She flew out of the bed and ran to him. "Oh, your poor leg! What happened?"

"I told you. I got lost, injured . . . all that."

"The details, David. Tell me the whole story!"

David sighed, pulled on his clothing and began talking. Eleanor curled up under the covers with him sitting beside her. While he talked, she held him.

"I went out, as you know, to be trained in the jungle. There was an instructor, two other trainees and myself. We came to a wide and tumbling river that we needed to cross. We went upstream, trying to find a way over. After a three day hike in which we made about five miles . . . those jungles are thick, Eleanor . . . we reached an escarpment we had to climb. The river fell in a beautiful cascade down the cliff, and at the top the instructor was sure he could see a chasm narrow enough to bridge.

"We made it up that escarpment all right and sure enough, the river had cut a deep, narrow groove into the top of the cliff. We managed to sling ropes across it and got to the other side. We were too far upstream, of course, so we had to back-track. It was when we were trying to get down the cliff that the accident occurred; we were roped together and one man slipped, pulling the rest of us with him. The instructor was killed, and the man who had slipped.

"The two of us who survived were both hurt. I had this," and he indicated his game leg, "and my buddy, Juan Mercado, had a

166

broken arm. It was a terrible fracture; the two bones of his forearm were snapped and protruding jaggedly through his skin. When we both regained consciousness, we were feverish and in a lot of pain. We both knew that if we just lay there waiting for help, we would die. Our supplies were gone, no food, no medicine. We both had wives with children on the way . . ." David was silent for a few moments and Eleanor held him strongly until he was ready to go on.

"Juan could walk, even though he had only one good arm. I had two good arms, but couldn't move unaided. Juan managed to hack down some small trees with the one knife we had, and some vines. I got a splint on his arm, then we put some of the trees together with braided vines and made a very make-shift raft. We finally got it into the water and somehow managed to get both of us onto it.

"We floated downstream until in some rapids it broke up. We were pretty weak by that time and our re-build job wasn't very successful. We just lay on that float, waiting for it to fall apart again, and when it did, Juan simply drifted off! He didn't even fight, Eleanor, and I couldn't get to him!"

The anguish in David's voice cut into his

wife like a hot knife. She held his head tightly to her breast and said, "That's enough, darling. No more."

"I want to finish! I got ashore by hanging onto one of the logs from the raft and pulled myself half out of the water. I don't know how long I lay there, but after a while some Indians found me and took me to their encampment. They looked after me for a long time . . . I think I spent seven months there before I could even begin to think about finding a way out. I didn't know who I was, where I was from, or what I was doing there. My whole world was like that of a baby who had been born to the tribe, full-grown, but reliant on them for everything. It took a further two months, after I became myself again, to convince them that they had to show me the way out. Finally, three of them agreed to take me back to civilisation.

"I was still sick when I got back to Lima, darling, and when I was finally well again, I knew I could never come back here . . ."

Eleanor remained silent for a long moment, still cradling his head against her. She let her hold slacken when he failed to continue with this, the most important part of his story. He pulled away from her and buried his face in his hands.

She had to ask! "Why?"

"I . . . can't tell you . . . Oh, darling, don't ask!"

"You must know it's a question I was bound to ask, David! A question which must be answered!" Oh, why was he holding back?

"But it's a question I cannot answer!" He raised a ravaged face to her, reaching out for her and she backed away from him to the other side of the bed. "Eleanor," he beseeched her, "believe me! I would tell you if I could!"

The screen door squeaked open, slammed, and Eleanor looked at David with hopeless, dead eyes. "The school bus is in. Phillip is home. Go and meet him. I'm sure he'll want to thank you for looking after his mother, Jeff."

"Jeff?" David whispered, agony in his eyes, his voice, his stance.

Eleanor swallowed with difficulty. She licked suddenly dry lips. "Yes. Jeff," she replied in a voice she barely recognised as her own. "Jeff." She turned her back on him.

EIGHT

David caught Eleanor by the shoulder and dragged her close to him. She stared up into his tense, white face. "Why?" he whispered.

"I think you can figure that out! If there can't be truth between us, what can there be?"

"He told me," David said rapidly, quietly, a note of desperation in his voice. "He told me that you said his father would have to have a good reason if he ever did come back . . . a good reason for having stayed away. But I have, Eleanor! I have!"

"Then tell . . ."

"Hey, Jeff! Where's my mom?" yelled Phillip as he ran across the kitchen and the hallway. "Oh, there you are. You all better Mom? You sounded funny and I couldn't find Kathy and Bill so I got up on Siwash and went to get the Exleys and then Jeff came home before I rode that far and he looked after you for me. Hey, Mom, how come your face is all red now? It was white last night."

Eleanor subsided back against her pillow

and David quickly thrust another behind her. "What . . . or who, is Siwash?" she asked, feeling more and more wretched with each passing moment.

"My horse," replied David tersely.

Her eyes flew from the face of her son to that of her husband. "He rode a horse?" she asked in awe.

"Sure, Mom! Me 'n' Casey've been riding on Si since Saturday. Jeff holds the reins and we walk around and around the clearing but when you got sick I had to do it all by myself! Can I go out and ride him again, Jeff? I like it now!"

David nodded and Phillip scampered off.

"His school clothes," Eleanor protested weakly, and Dave called the boy back.

"Change into your play clothes, sport, won't you? If you fall down you might get your good things all dirty and I know you wouldn't want to do that, especially when your mom's sick. Let's you and me try to keep the laundry to a minimum. O.K.?" David smiled into the child's face as he spoke, then ruffled the tow-head.

"O.K., Jeff," replied Phillip cheerfully. "Are you going to cook dinner tonight, or is Mom?"

Before Eleanor could assure her son that she was quite capable of preparing dinner, a lie, and she knew it, David's hard hand pushed her back into the pillows. "I am," he said. "Your mom's still feeling kind of bad, Phil, and I've managed to keep her in bed most of the day." He let what Eleanor chose to call a dirty smirk flit across his face for a moment, then went on. "She needs all the rest she can get. Want any help mounting Si, or do you want to do it alone by climbing up from the fence?"

"I'll do it my ownself!" sang the boy as he sauntered from the room, flinging clothes helter-skelter as he went.

"Hang up your pants!" called David.

"Aw, Jeff! You sound just like my mom!"

David stood there looking down at Eleanor's back which had been turned to him during this last exchange between father and son. He remained silent until he heard the screen door slam shut. "Darling, look at me," he ordered quietly.

Eleanor might have been made of stone.

David sat down beside her on the bed and a tremor ran through her as his weight depressed the springs and rolled her toward him. He put his hands on her shoulders and pulled her around to face him. She squeezed her eyes tightly shut, could feel her mouth trembling, tried to stop it and failed. She gave up the struggle then, and opened her eyes, knowing he would know about the tears she was trying to hide even if she did keep them covered with squeezed eyelids.

"Go home, David."

"I am home, Eleanor," and the old, caressing note was in his tone as he said her name. "This is my home. You are my wife. We proved that today. No matter what, we belong together. Phillip is our son and together we are a family. I built this house, remember?"

"I remember," she whispered. "But I also remember more than seven years of silence, seven years of raising my son alone. I remember the years of watching my father slowly die, having to bury him alone, without my husband beside me to give me support when I needed it. I was so alone when Dad died, Dave, and for the next four years I just barely made it. All that held me together was Phillip, my writing, and living with the hope that you would, by some miracle, return. Well here you are, David. You have returned. The miracle did happen and when I ask you how it happened . . . why . . . all you can say is you remember building this house.

"What else do you remember, David? You told me that for months you didn't know who you were, where you were, or why you were there. What happened during that time, David? What else do you remember? A woman . . . dark hair and eyes, some children, perhaps, whom you couldn't bear to leave? Seven years is a long time, David, and you won't convince me you didn't make a life for yourself . . . either before or after you decided that Phillip and I could have no place in the one you had. Another thing I would like to know is why have you left them now? Why did you come back? Did whomever it was kept you away for so long finally make you leave?"

His face was grey, drawn. "Is that what you believe?"

"You give me no choice but to draw my own conclusions! That seems most l-log-i-cal!" And she choked on the last word, put her hands into her hair, rolled on her side and shook with paroxysms of grief, grief which David knew could only be assuaged by words he dared not utter; for to do so would be to cause a wound that even he, given time, might never be able to heal, as he hoped to heal this wound she was aching from now. All he could do was hold her, hold her and hope that the same miracle which had sent him back here would give him the time with her he needed to make her believe that his reason, unspoken though it must remain, was the best.

"Go away . . . go away . . ." she moaned. "I can't bear you to touch me!"

"Stop this! Oh, God, Eleanor! Stop!"

"Go!"

And he went, but only to find more aspirins. "Take these. You're burning up again. Take them and sleep some more. I'll look after everything."

"I know! I know!" she wept distractedly. "And it frightens me! Grant looked after everything, too, because I was sick, and in spite of the way he was . . . is with Phillip, I agreed to start proceedings to have you declared dead . . . so I could *marry* him, David! But you aren't dead, and I'm married to you! And I love you so much! I'll never marry Grant now, but I don't know if I can stay married to you, because for all those years you might have been dead and suddenly here you are, looking after me, looking after my son, giving us both orders and making us like it, teaching Phillip to ride, ridding him of his fear of horses and what if I feel for you is the same as what I felt for Grant . . . gratitude that someone, anyone, has taken over and let me rest when I needed to?"

He held her tenderly as she wept and ranted, and when she was finished, he gave her a little shake and pulled her face up to look down into her puffy eyes. "Sweetheart," he said seriously, "did you go to bed with Grant when you were feeling grateful to him?"

"Of course not! I don't lo . . ."

"No. You don't love him. You love me, and after the loving we shared today, can you say you might just feel gratitude to me?"

"I don't know! I don't know! You aren't the same. You don't even look the same; your face is all hidden, you're bigger around, so much more muscled!" What she said did not seem to be making much sense, but David answered as if it did to him.

"You married a boy, Eleanor. He has simply become a man through the intervening years. You loved me before, when I was skinny and underfed, so why shouldn't you love me still, when I look more mature? Why do you have to feel guilty about choosing me over Grant simply because I'm more of a man in your eyes? You chose me long before you ever knew of his existence."

"Is that what I'm feeling?"

"I think so, darling."

"But where did you grow from the boy into the man?" And with whom? she wanted to ask. In whose company? But something held her back. When she had suggested it before, he had not denied it!

"We have a long time ahead of us, sweet lady, to catch up on all that . . . if you will just give me that time! Time to teach you to trust me again. I promise I will tell you all the places I've been, all the jobs I've done, but you will just have to accept, for now, the fact that my reason for not returning was the best in the world, the only one that would ever have kept me from you. And accept that I have returned and will never leave you and Phillip again unless you send me away. Can you accept me on those terms, Eleanor?"

Her heart thundered out the word, Yes! It screamed through her blood, her body and her mind. It seemed to be lighting her eyes from within, lightning the darkness of misery which had been the only thing David had seen for the past few minutes. His heart leapt in his breast as she leaned toward him, her lips half parted.

Eleanor closed her eyes for a second as she swayed toward David, then something jerked her back and she opened her eyes, looked straight into his slate-grey ones and said, "No."

David bowed his head then picked up her left hand. With gentle, slow, movements, he held it to his lips, kissed each finger-tip one by one then kissed the golden band he had placed there so long before. Still bowed over her nerveless hand, he placed a finger and thumb over the band and gently removed it from her. He put it in his shirt pocket. Still without meeting her eyes, he said in a dull, lifeless voice, "As soon as you want to, we'll go into town and see a lawyer."

Eleanor stared into the empty space where David had been sitting, then at the white band of skin around her finger for a long time after David had gently closed the door behind him. Then she turned and wept silently into her pillow until she slept.

The following morning when she awoke, it was to hear the screen door slam and Phillip calling, "See you later, Jeff! Look after my measley little mom for me!"

"Sure will, sport. So long!" came the cheerful, not at all heart-broken reply from Eleanor's husband.

How did I suddenly become nothing more than a 'measley little mom'? she wondered, feeling hurt. Has David been preaching ideas about the 'weaker sex' . . . 'the little woman'? She felt horrible! Ordinarily something like that coming from her son wouldn't bother her, she knew, but after the terrible night she had just put in, with fever, chills and nightmares, everything was going to bother her today. She slipped out of the bed and padded to the window. She swooped the drapes open and the bright sun stabbed into her eyes, making them ache like nothing else on earth!

Eleanor put a hand to her burning face and as she turned to go into the bathroom the act of putting one foot in front of the other made her head throb unbearably. She coughed deep in her chest and it seemed to be tearing her very lungs out. Moaning slightly from the pain in her eyes, in her head and chest and all her joints, Eleanor washed her face, hoping to cool it. As she reached for a towel on the rack, she saw a shaving kit standing large as life, and looking like it belonged, on the toilet tank.

With a wild sweep of her hand, she sent it flying across the room. The lid off the spray can of lather clattered into the tub and the door burst open to reveal David standing there, a look of fear on his face.

"What happened?" he barked. Then, "Oh. I thought you'd fallen." He gave a glance at the debris from his shaving kit littering the floor, then reached out a gentle hand to his wife. "Come on, sweetheart, back to bed. Finished in here?"

Dumbly, she nodded, then holding onto

the side of the basin, said, "But you have to leave! You shouldn't have brought your shaving gear here! Why did you cut off the beard? Now you're David, my David again!" She sobbed, holding her face in her hands, and said, "Oh, please go away!"

"I can't leave you like this, Eleanor. Look in the mirror . . ." David twisted her face around until she was forced to see her reflection.

"No . . ." she groaned. "Oh, no!"

"Oh, yes. Oh, yes indeed! Now back to bed with you and when I close the drapes, you leave 'em that way." He steered her into the bedroom, put her in bed and tucked the blankets securely around her. "Shame on you, Eleanor, not getting the measles vaccine for yourself when you had Phillip immunised. I've already called the doctor and he'll be by in a little while."

"How . . . how did you call the doctor?" she asked weakly, feeling the tears still trickling down her cheeks, but powerless to stop them.

"I asked Bill if I could use his phone. Phillip told me that's what you did," David explained patiently.

"Y-you've m-met Bill? What . . . ?"

"Did I tell him about myself? Only that I've bought the Anderson place, made friends with Phillip and that when you got sick and he wasn't home, Phil came to me. He's gone back to the hospital to be with his wife and babies. He says he won't tell Kathy about your measles as she'd only worry. O.K.?"

Eleanor had no answer.

The doctor came, went, and Eleanor slept. For the next few days she spent more time that way than she did awake, but she was aware now and then of David coming in and out of the room, giving her cold drinks, bits of food, feeding her aspirins and once, only once, bathing her again in the night when the fever became too high.

She would call him, and he was there. She vaguely wondered where he was sleeping; it must be in the living room, for he did not share her bed. It did not occur to her that he was only snatching the odd cat-nap when he could, and that he was doing that in the big chair at her bedside.

He changed her bedding and night-clothes when she perspired so much they became soaked, but the one time she became so cold that she begged and pleaded with him for warmth, he only wrapped her in a scratchy wool blanket and put hot water bottles beside her. She cried to him to come to her, to make her warm, but he said sadly,

"No, darling. You're ill, and if I had known how ill, that first time, what happened, wouldn't have. Sleep now, and we'll talk about it again when you're better."

Eleanor was sitting up in bed a week after her spots had first appeared. They were beginning to fade now, and her eyes felt so much better that David had left the drapes open a few inches, letting a golden splotch of sunlight fall across her green carpet. She heard steps in the yard, then rapping at the kitchen door.

David's heavy footsteps went slowly, haltingly across the hall and into the kitchen. He sounds so weary, she thought with contrition as she heard the screen door squeak open. David said to the caller, "Good morning. I'll have to oil that door! Squeaks something awful, doesn't it?"

And Grant . . . Grant! answered, "Who the hell are you? Where's Mrs. Jefferson?"

"Oh, she's still in bed," replied David easily, a chuckle in his voice, an indulgent, tender little chuckle! "I've been keeping her there as much as possible."

"You've what? Who are you?" Grant barked.

"Oh, yes . . . of course, you don't know, do you?" asked David in an apologetic manner. Eleanor held her breath and let it out in a long sigh of . . . relief . . . ? disappointment . . . ? when he went on. "I'm Jeff Davidson, a friend of young Phillip. He came to me for help when his mother got sick. She has the measles," he added with casual cruelty. But how could it be cruelty? Eleanor thought. He doesn't know about how Grant fears illness! Unless . . . Phillip . . . ? Or herself, even, in her delirium . . . ?

If he hadn't known, if the casual cruelty had been lucky accident, he would have known in the next instant, Eleanor decided, for Grant's voice rose a full octave as he said, "Measles?" with such horror that she wondered how he would have reacted to small-pox!

David replied with pleasure, it sounded. "Yes, measles. Red measles. The bad kind. What did you say your name was?" He knows very well! thought Eleanor indignantly. He saw us together!

"I didn't. I'm Mrs. Jefferson's fiance, Grant Appleton."

"Oh, I am glad to see you! She's been very ill, you know, been calling out for some man or other in her delirium. Come right in! Let me show you to her bedroom!" David offered effusively.

"I know where it is," snapped Grant testily. "But I don't think I sh . . ."

"Nonsense!" said David heartily. Too heartily, his wife snarled mentally. "She'll be longing to see you and she's so much better she must be getting bored with my constant company, day and night. Go right on in and give her a big kiss! Don't mind me, all I am is house-maid, nurse, chief cook and bottle-washer. I'll make coffee for the two of you."

He ushered Grant through the open doorway and stood behind him, blocking off all exit. "Heh-heh," laughed falsely. "I understand from the kid's friend that you have measles, Ellie. How did that happen?"

Before Eleanor could answer, David's big, flat palm clapped Grant right between the shoulder blades, sending him staggering into the middle of the room, while David said, "Go on, man! That poor girl's been missing you a lot. She's spent the last few nights calling for 'darling, darling' to make her warm. She must have meant you, so for heaven's sake go and do it!"

Grant pulled himself up short. "I . . . uh, look, Ellie . . . if I get too close I might catch them . . . the motel, you know . . . the guests . . ."

He looked so miserable standing there,

afraid to approach too near her, and even more afraid to retreat, because David might push him again, that Eleanor had to take pity on him. She smiled. "I understand, Grant."

"Well I don't," said David, an evil gleam in his eye. "What's more important, the girl you supposedly love, or a bunch of motel guests who probably had the disease as children or at least had sense enough to get themselves immunised?"

"Well!" blustered Grant, puffing his cheeks out. "Just who do you think you are, anyway?"

"No one," replied Dave, "except the person who has nursed this woman through a very serious illness, and I feel that every consideration should be given her. If she wants you to kiss her, then I think you should."

Grant drew himself up to his not very great full height and glared at David. "If Mrs. Jefferson understands the importance of the safety of the guests, I'd think you, a relative stranger, could keep out of it!"

"That's me!" David shot a nasty little grin at Eleanor. "A relative-stranger, wouldn't you say, Mrs. Jefferson?"

She glared at him, speechless, and Grant filled the gap in conversation. "I'll see to it that you're well paid for your troubles, and if you'd make that coffee now, I'm sure Mrs. Jefferson would appreciate it. I always use that large, blue mug in the cupboard above the stove. I like lots of coffee, and I like it strong!"

Eleanor was hard put to lie still and not run screaming from the room, screaming with laughter, at David's next words: "The blue mug? Would that be the one Phillip has been using to mix the dog mash in, Mrs. Jefferson?" Without waiting for a reply, he almost bowed and ducked out of the room.

When David had been and gone, serving the coffee with a deference at which Eleanor had great difficulty keeping a straight face, Grant leaned back in the chair, keeping well away from her she noticed.

"Have you done anything about getting your freedom?" he asked complacently expecting an affirmative reply, she realised.

"I've been sick, Grant," she said to avoid a direct reply. "I've hardly been out of this bed for days. I wasn't expecting you back yet anyway."

"I managed to finish up sooner than I expected," he replied, and reached for his coffee. He set it down quickly again, without having sipped, and shuddered. So

David's little dart about the dog mash, untrue as Eleanor knew it to be, had struck home. "I'm glad to see you aren't wearing your wedding ring any more, Eleanor. It makes me hope you really mean business this time . . ."

"Grant," she interrupted him, "there's something I think I should t . . ."

"Mrs. Jefferson, will Mr. Applebaum be staying for lunch?" David's eyes were dancing with an unholy glee as he bounded into the room, not pausing to knock on the door which he had left ajar after serving the coffee. Eleanor knew he'd been lurking out there in the hall, eavesdropping!

"No!" cried Grant. "That is . . . I . . . the dishes . . . I can't take that much . . ." He broke off lamely.

"Risk?" supplied David politely. "The dishes might have germs on them?" He glanced at Grant's still-full coffee mug. "Oh, Mr. Appletree! Was the coffee not to your liking?"

"No," replied Grant. "And the name is Appleton. After all, Ellie," he pleaded with her for understanding, "this man's not a properly trained nurse . . . he can't know about sterilising and . . . all that . . . That's it! Ellie, I'll send a nurse out . . . this afternoon!"

"No thanks, Appleton." David's voice was hard, all traces of mockery were gone from it. "I've gone on this far looking after Mrs. Jefferson and Phillip, and I will continue to do so until she tells me my . . . services . . . are no longer required." The deliberate hesitation over the word 'services', was accompanied by that nasty, dirty little smirk of David's and Eleanor wanted to throw something at him. Something heavy! Something hard!

"Surely," Grant said stiffly, "it's up to me to decide what's best for my fiancée, and to her, of course," he added with a quick glance at Eleanor.

"Certainly," agreed David pleasantly. "Mrs. Jefferson?"

There was no hesitation in her answer. "I'd rather not have a nurse, thank you Grant. Phillip is used to having things the way they are, and after all, he went out alone at night, and rode a horse, as frightened as he is . . . was . . . of horses, to get help for me. To change things now would only make him think I don't appreciate what he did for me."

"Always the kid," said Grant. "What about showing me a little of that appreciation?" He shrugged petulantly and got to his feet. "Oh, well, at least you took off that damned ring. I guess I can't expect to wean you away from all parts of your past at once."

"Do you expect to wean me away from my son?" asked Eleanor, dangerously quiet and with raised brows.

"No, no! Of course not!" Grant hastened to assure her. "But I am glad to see that ring gone!"

David spoke quietly from just inside the doorway. Grant looked over his shoulder at him, surprised to see the other man still there. "I took the ring off her when she was ill," he said. "It seemed to be an irritation to her." He approached the bed, dropped to one knee in front of Eleanor, and holding her eyes with his own, he slowly unbuttoned his shirt pocket and extracted the ring. He held it in front of her on the palm of his hand. It glittered in the sunlight. "Would you like it back on, Mrs. Jefferson?" asked David quietly.

Eleanor wrenched her eyes from David's and stared down at the bright circlet of gold on the broad, work-toughened hand. It was so fragile, so delicate, this bond between them, and she ached with all her heart and soul to be able to ask him to replace it. But . . .

"Not . . . just yet," she whispered. "Thank

you, D . . . Jeff."

"All right," he replied softly, looking deep into her pain-filled brown and amber eyes with complete understanding and love. "All right." Then, standing, he tucked the ring back into his pocket, buttoned the flap and said briskly, "I think Mrs. Jefferson is tired now, so I'll leave you to make your tender farewells." He spun on his heel and marched out, banging the door solidly behind him.

Grant stood looking bewildered for a moment and then said with a hollow laugh, "A very strange man, that friend of the kid's. How come he put your ring back into his pocket? What's wrong with your jewellery box?"

Eleanor thought desperately for an answer. She was tired, and she wished Grant would go! She knew an explanation would have to be made, but not now. The time for that had been when she had begun to make it, back then when David had broken in on them. Deliberately? And if so, why? Still, she was too tired, feeling too sick to try to explain it to Grant now. She would be unequal to the ensuing battle. All she could think of to say about the ring was, "I imagine he feels it's safer there and it will be easier for him to give it back to me if I

190

should ask for it, than if he had to dig through the mess in my jewellery box."

"Are you going to ask for it back?" asked Grant in a hard voice.

"I don't know . . . I'm not sure, Grant," she whispered and he spun on his heel as David had done and walked rapidly out of the room. I'm not being fair to him, she thought anguishedly, but I really couldn't have faced an argument today!

David avoided her room for the rest of the day except for bringing and collecting her lunch tray, and the next time Eleanor heard his voice was when Phillip came home from school. The screen door slammed . . . without having squeaked open first! Phillip, too, noticed the difference at once. "Hey!" he exclaimed. "The door doesn't squeak!"

"No," rumbled David's voice. "I oiled it. Like a lot of things around here, my son, it's been needing a man's attention for a long time."

NINE

Needing a man's attention? Eleanor asked herself. Meaning exactly what? Me? Phillip? And thereby saying by implication that Grant was not a man? It must be admitted, she thought, that Grant had given a very poor showing of himself today, and she had been ashamed of him, of his fear of infection, of his patronisation of David, whom he took to be nothing more than a working-class flunky to be sent out to the kitchen to make coffee, to be offered money for his services.

But David had shown himself more than capable of looking after himself! A smile twitched at the corners of her mouth as she remembered, and she wiped it away quickly, feeling guilty that she had been so amused, even while feeling angry, at what he had done to poor, unsuspecting Grant.

To imply that Grant was not a man was unfair. He, at least, had been loyal, steadfast, and had stuck with Eleanor for four long years, knowing it would be a long wait until she was free, and not knowing if the wait would be worth it in the long run. But I never asked him to wait! she told herself. I always told him I was unsure, and that it might be better if he forgot me!

But Grant had always kept coming back, and in doing so, had proved that he must care for her very deeply! He had taken an interest in her work, believed in her enough to send it to his brother with his personal recommendation! Surely all that counted for something, and even if he had appeared a little on the mercenary side, it was only that that was the way of his personality. He can't help being the way he is, and I'm sure, if I were going to marry him, he would never have insisted on evicting Bill, so we could keep the profits of the farm for ourselves. He's a businessman . . . doesn't understand sentiment. If it hadn't been for his ambition, he wouldn't have gotten to where he is, so David is most unfair to say he's not man enough! But I wonder what I should do about the farm? Keep renting it . . . offer it to Bill . . . ?

I'll have to ask David . . . David. Yes. It always comes back to David in the end, for I love him in spite of his having been gone so long. I try to tell myself that I don't trust him, yet when I feel insecure, undecided, I have an immediate need to ask him what to do. He must have plans for Phillip's future; if he hadn't he wouldn't have come back so I won't need to have the farm hanging around my neck like a mill stone! I can support myself, as long as I have financial help for Phillip . . .

"Is my mom better, Jeff?" Phillip's voice, sounding full of cookies, broke into her reverie.

"Almost," was the reply. "Why don't you go and see her . . . ask her what she wants for dinner."

Phillip came into her bedroom exuding an energy which crackled and snapped in his eyes, filling the air with boy. He landed on the bed with a bounce and a whoop and the springs protested loudly. "Hi, Mom! What you want to eat?"

Eleanor gave him a hug. He looked so happy, so full of life and good spirits and the joy of knowing that the two people whom he loved best in all the world were together in the same house. She squeezed him tightly for an instant, feeling love rush over her in a wave almost painful. Phillip struggled and she let him go, saying, "Never mind me. What would you like for supper?"

"Hamburgers and chips. Jeff c'n make 'em. He can make anything! Did you get some of that Jello he made? It was the nicest Jello, Mom. He let me drink it out of a cup!

How come you never make Jello like that?"

Eleanor grinned in spite of herself. *He can make anything, can he?* "I didn't know you'd appreciate drinkable Jello, Phillip, and if you ask Jeff, he'll probably make hamburgers and chips for you. But tell him that you have to eat some vegetables, too. I'm not hungry, and certainly not for drinkable Jello!"

"Fink!" said David from the doorway and Phillip jumped up, giving Eleanor's message in his normally shrill, loud tones, then finished by saying, without pausing for breath, "What's 'fink'?"

"That's someone who tells on someone else," replied David. "And do you absolutely have to yell? I thought that Jello was a secret between you and me!" He gave Eleanor a sheepish grin over the boy's head and her heart flipped painfully before she managed to steel it against his charm.

"Oh," said Phillip airily, "we don't have to keep secrets from Mom. We can tell her all that stuff. She understands."

David stared long and sadly at Eleanor. *Oh, no she doesn't,* his eyes seemed to be saying, and she met his gaze, held it, her eyes in turn assuring him that she did . . . she would understand, if he would only give her something to understand. *Trust me!*

She pleaded silently, and his gaze dropped first. "I'm sure she does, son," said David to Phillip, but his words were directed to Eleanor and she knew it. "I would never keep anything from your mother if I could help it. But . . ." and he raised his eyes to Eleanor once more, ". . . there are some things which told, would do more damage than the silence of not telling them."

Both adults seemed to have forgotten the child as they looked with pain and longing at one another's eyes, the man begging for mercy, for understanding, the woman seeking knowledge, trust, truth. "How can you be sure of that unless you try?" she asked.

Casey, at that moment, bounded into the room, his claws clicking on the hardwood surrounding the rug and he skidded against Phillip's legs. The child reached down and picked him up, giggling as the small pink tongue attacked his ear. "Take him out for a little run, please, Phillip," said David, and when the child had gone, he sat down and took Eleanor's hands.

"When I was away, I thought of you every day," he said. "I never stopped missing you, never stopped loving you. I used to take out my little snap-shot of you and look at it every day, and every night before I slept, until one night when I was in prison for a crime I did not commit, the rats ate it. Even after that I carried a picture of you in my heart. You are my life, my love, and always have been. But I can't tell you what kept me away. You hurt yourself, Eleanor, and me, and Phillip, too, by refusing to trust me. If I thought it would help you to know, believe me, I would tell you. But I know it would be the worst possible thing to do." He leaned forward and placed his head against her breast, and of their own volition, her fingers tangled in his hair. "Trust me," he whispered.

"Do you trust me?" she asked, hardly daring to breathe.

"I trust you with my life."

"Then tell me."

David stood up. "Impasse," he said sadly. "What would you like for dinner?"

"Nothing."

"I'll bring you something. You'll eat it."

"I'll get up and eat in the kitchen with you and Phillip. He'll like that, since it will be your last night here."

"Will it?"

"Yes, David."

That night, after the dinner for three in the kitchen . . . a bitter-sweet affair for the two adults, and fun-time for Phillip . . . the dishes were done, put away, the kitchen tidied and Phillip tucked into bed before David left.

Eleanor sat alone in the twilit living room, looking out at the night approaching fast and wondered how many more nights of aloneness she would be having. How quiet the house was . . . how empty! David's presence had been what the small cottage had needed, and now it was gone, gone by her doing! She had sent him away . . .

While Eleanor sat in her lonely, empty little house, with her lonely, empty thoughts, her husband sat on a canvas chair under the stars beside his camper on the forestry road.

I'll give her two weeks, he told himself. If she hasn't come to me by then, I will tell her what she wants to know, though God alone knows what it will do to her! She's still too sick, too weak, to cope with that knowledge yet, and I cannot do it to her!

Grant sat in his office, slowly sipping his fifth rye and ginger of the evening, wondering why it tasted so bad, and thinking back to the odd morning he had spent at Ellie's place. What a strange man that had been! Grant felt uneasy, and couldn't have said why. All he knew was that something in him kept whispering, "You've lost! You've lost!" Oh, no I have not! he told the voice. I will never give up!

By Friday evening the voice inside was beginning to worry Grant. He went to her house at a time when he knew the kid would be in bed.

"Oh . . . it's you," was her greeting, and he pushed in to the doorway, suddenly fearing she might try to keep him out.

"I take it you're alone?" he asked.

"Yes, I'm alone, except, of course, for Phillip and Casey."

"That man?"

"He left on Tuesday night. He went back to his camper." Eleanor heard herself say it so calmly, and wondered how she could do it. It was like being calm and trying to say the world fell in half on Tuesday; the other side is going out to orbit another sun.

"That's good! Listen, Ellie, I'm glad he's gone, because quite frankly, if he'd still been here, I'd have been forced to ask him to leave. I did some checking in town this week, and I don't like what I've found out."

"Oh?" said Eleanor on a note of enquiry, "what kind of checking?" I should tell him!

"Did you know the man has been hanging around here since before Easter? He arrived one morning, and right away began asking questions. He was driving a brand-new car, wearing what looked like very, very expensive clothing, and the first thing he did was go into the post office . . . his excuse was to buy two airmail stamps, but what he really wanted to do, and did do, was pump Charlie. I talked to Charlie, and he said that right from the first he had doubts about the man."

"Just what did Charlie have to say?" asked Eleanor, knowing she was going to have to tell Grant the truth tonight, but somehow, for some odd reason, she wanted to know what David had done when he first arrived. Of course David would realise that Charlie Simmons, the garrulous postmaster would be the best source of information in town. He would surely have remembered that much!

"Well, it seems there was no one in the post office and this Davidson guy, if that is his name," doubt was oozing from Grant's tone, "just leaned on the counter and started asking questions about old-timers. He claimed to have lived here for a few months, years ago, although Charlie doesn't remember him. They got to talking about who was still alive, who had passed on, and when your old man was mentioned, he wanted to know right away who was farming the place. Charlie told him it was Bill Robins.

"I asked Charlie if he'd mentioned you and the kid to the guy, and the fact that you were sort of isolated down here in this little hollow, and he denied it. Said the guy hadn't asked about you, so he figured Davidson hadn't ever met you."

"Why did you wonder if he'd asked about me . . . us?"

"Well, because of the way he'd buddied up to the kid sort of right after he bought the Anderson place. I thought maybe he had some ulterior motive."

"What ulterior motive could there be for befriending a little boy?"

"Oh, Ellie. Come on!"

Eleanor snorted. She couldn't help it. What Grant was suggesting was too ridiculous!

"Now just a minute!" Grant protested. "Don't take that attitude with me! It has happened, you know, and the man did act suspiciously. After he found out about your dad, and that Bill was farming the place, he started asking about other properties in the district, implying that he was in the market. Charlie told him about the Anderson place, that it had been listed for years and no one seemed to want it. He got really pleased looking, Charlie said, and went off to see Rick Forrest. Charlie got the rest of the story from Katie, Rick's secretary."

The realtor wouldn't be too happy to hear about that! thought Eleanor, raising her brows in encouragement for Grant to go on.

"This Davidson fellow went away for a few days and then came back and bought the Anderson place from Rick. Ellie, he paid cash!"

She widened her eyes to show astonishment, knowing she was being most nasty in playing like this with Grant, but unable to stop. "My," she said, impressed. "Cash?"

"Yes. Cash!" It was a dirty word the way Grant said it. "Makes you wonder, doesn't it, just where all that cash came from? That place didn't go cheap; Rick says that's why he had it on his books for so long, and he was so happy to get rid of it, he didn't ask any questions, and gave the guy a rebate, as well!" Rick Forrest had obviously fallen in Grant's estimation, and he shrugged, continuing.

"Not only had he the cash to pay for the place, but he'd got rid of the flashy car, the expensive stuff, and showed up in a new camper, wearing work-clothes. Charlie says, and he's a pretty shrewd judge of character, that there's something funny in all that. First, the guy throws money around like he has a tree of it in his back yard, then all of a sudden he pulls in his horns and begins to live almost like a tramp. Charlie thought maybe the guy figured he was making too big a splash and scared himself, so decided to lay low for a few months."

"Lay low?" asked Eleanor, knowing quite well what Grant was getting at, but taking an odd pleasure in poking secret fun at him, just as David had done that morning. But why should I be acting like this? I was furious when David did the same thing . . . Wasn't I?

"Yes. Lay low," repeated Grant. "When a man comes into a new district, saying nothing about himself, where he's from, what his line of work is, and asks questions about who's alive and who's not, then buys up a secluded farm with no really near neighbours . . . you're the nearest, Ellie, and you're separated from him by the hill and the wood-lot, unless you want to drive around the five miles of the big bend in the highway . . . Where was I? Oh, yes, well when a man does all that, and then all of a sudden begins acting like an itinerant worker, no one could be blamed for thinking he'd come by all his cash dishonestly, and may be planning to get some more of it, just as dishonestly!"

"Oh! Maybe he's a counterfeiter? Or a bank robber? Is that what you're thinking?"

"It wasn't me thinking those things, Ellie, so there's no need to be sarcastic. It was Charlie!" replied Grant huffily.

"But you must have agreed with him, Grant, or you wouldn't have come prepared to throw him out." The picture of Grant doing that to David was so ludicrous, too funny to contemplate! She pushed it out of her mind.

"Well . . ." said Grant reluctantly, "it did seem a bit odd, I mean after Charlie pointed out all this to me. I started worrying about you . . . and the kid, of course!"

"Of course," murmured Eleanor dryly.

"You show so little sense, Ellie! You knew nothing at all about the man, yet you've been letting the kid hang around with him all this time, and even let him come into your home when you were sick!"

"But if you'll remember, I thought he was an imaginary friend, until he did come into my home, and at that point, I was too sick to do any arguing about it."

"But you let him stay, Ellie, when I offered you a nurse to replace him! What kind of sense does that make?"

"None at all, Grant, except that he's my husband."

"Of course none at all . . . He's your WHAT?"

"My husband, Grant. David Jefferson," she replied baldly.

"Christ! What do we do now?"

"I don't know, Grant. I honestly don't know. I was sitting here trying to figure that out when you came. I let you go on telling me about him in the hopes that it would give me some clues about him."

Grant got to his feet, walked to the liquor cabinet, poured himself a stiff rye and drank it down straight. He poured another, then looked over at Eleanor. "Want one?" She shook her head.

"I'll get you some ice," she said, taking the glass from him and going into the kitchen to give Grant a few minutes alone to pull himself together. *I should have led up to it somehow,* she berated herself. *I shouldn't have just blurted it out like that! But he made me so mad suggesting all those things about David!*

She returned and gave Grant the glass with three ice cubes bobbing in the whiskey. He took it without thanks and sat back down. "Well," he said again, "what do we do now?"

"I don't know, Grant," Eleanor replied as she had done before.

"Why? Why in God's name did he come back after all this time?"

"I don't know that, either. He says, because he loves me."

"Where has he been? Why did he stay away so long . . . he obviously wasn't dead!"

Eleanor's silence was eloquent, and Grant went on more quietly. "Ellie, have you asked him any of those questions?"

"Yes."

"And he didn't tell you?"

"No."

"Then what are we doing sitting here like this? You've got to divorce him, Ellie! You simply must now!"

"Not at ten o'clock in the evening, Grant," she replied wearily. "I have to think it out."

"There can't be anything to think about!" he yelled. "Ellie, listen to me! If he won't even tell you where he's been, why he didn't come back, you can't still want him!"

"Can't I?" she asked bitterly.

"No!" was the positive reply. "You may think you do, and it's understandable; he's been your dream for all these years, but dreamtime's over, Ellie. Face facts! If he had loved you, he would have returned! I've

206

invested four years of my time waiting for you to get free of him, and I'm damned if I'll sit still and let him have you back after the way he's treated you! What he's done is the most reprehensible thing a man can do! He walked out on you and then when he decided to come back, he made up to the kid first so you wouldn't have a leg to stand on. After all, what Phillip wants, Phillip gets!"

"Now hold on, Grant! I have never given my son everything he ever wanted! He is not spoiled as you would have everyone believe! You are the only person in the world he's failed to take to, and that's more your fault than it is his. As far as I'm concerned, Grant, this is the best moment to tell you that I will not be marrying you!"

Grant, forgetting germs, measles, the 'travelling public', moved with bull-dog determination to Eleanor, caught her under the arms and lifted her into a tight embrace. His face was but an inch from hers as he grated, "You don't mean that! You only said it because you're upset and angry. I won't take no for an answer, Ellie! You are my woman and don't you forget it! You had what . . . ? a month with that man . . . as his wife, and you only knew him a few months before that. We've had four years, Ellie, and I think you owe me something for those, if nothing else! I'll give you one week in which to make up your mind!" He kissed her brutally hard on the mouth and strode off angrily into the night.

The weekend was long and dismal for Eleanor. Her son and the puppy spent every waking hour with David and she was left to recover her strength by sitting in the rose arbour brooding. The dull hum of the bees droning in the scented air, the warmth of the June sun and the residue of weakness from her days in bed made any profound thoughts difficult to hold onto.

She worried over her conversation with Grant on the Friday evening. What he had said was true. She must owe him something for those four years . . . mustn't she? Not love, no. That she did not have for him, but consideration . . . ? Respect . . . ? She owed him both of those, perhaps, and to be quite fair, she owed neither to David.

Yet her heart told her that she owed David to Phillip. Her son deserved the father whom he loved above everything, herself included she sometimes thought, even if the child did not know that the man he called 'Jeff' was his father. He would have to know, sooner or later!

Something else Grant had mentioned popped into her mind: Phillip in what seemed like a horrifyingly short time, would be leaving her. If she continued to find it impossible to accept David back on his terms . . . and she knew she would never marry Grant, regardless of what he said, then she was in for a good many long, lonely years.

These thoughts, and more like them, kept her company all weekend, except for a brief spell on Sunday afternoon when she moved out to the shade of an apple tree in the small orchard near the cottage.

David, determined, it seemed, to go on making the improvements on the place which he had claimed needed a man's attention, was cutting the long grass with a scythe.

The grass under the trees was in a deplorable condition, Eleanor had to admit. She hadn't trimmed it since early spring when it first began to grow. She sat and watched David working with her father's old scythe, making steady progress in neat swaths from tree to tree. It was the sweet scent of the newly-cut grass which was bringing the lump to her throat, she thought, not the sight of the smooth muscles rippling under David's dark skin, or the sight of her son working sturdily beside him. Phillip was using a sickle, trimming near the trunks of the trees where David could not go with the big scythe.

While they worked, David talked to the boy. "Take it easy, sport. Slow and easy. If you take gouges out of the bark it hurts the trees."

"Will they bleed? Do trees have blood?"

"In a way. It's called 'sap' and they need it just like we need blood. It's what keeps them alive."

Phillip looked worried. "That tree I nicked, is it going to die now?"

"No, silly!" laughed David, wiping the worried look from Phillip's face. "Do you die from a little cut on the finger?"

"No, but I hurt."

"The same with trees. Cut them a little, and they hurt a little. Cut them right down, and they die."

"But Jeff! What about the trees we cut down to make the cabin? They all died!" The boy was near to tears and Eleanor made a move to go to him. For the first time, David acknowledged her presence; he waved a hand at her to keep out of this!

He leaned his scythe up into a tree, took the sickle from Phillip and led him to the shady spot near . . . but not very near . . . Eleanor. She felt hurt, unaccountably left out, as David began talking to the child.

"Son, each kind of tree has a different use,

and I believe each tree knows it." Conviction rang in his tones. "The ones we cut down to make the cabin knew they were meant to grow tall and strong and straight so they could be turned into houses and furniture, just as these trees here," he gestured to the apple trees, "know that they were meant to stand here in the sun and grow apples for us to eat. Maple trees make big leaves to give us shade, and in the colder parts of the country, give a special sap that is turned into syrup for your hot-cakes. The dogwoods know their purpose on earth is to grow those white flowers just to look pretty and give people pleasure. So don't feel badly about the trees we cut down to make the cabin; they like being a house for people to live in."

"Just like Christmas trees don't mind being put in a house and decorated?"

"Just so, Phillip. They know that's the way it is."

"And Siwash doesn't mind us sitting on his back, and Casey doesn't mind sleeping on the porch, 'cause they know that's the way it has to be?"

"Exactly! You're smart." David ruffled the little boy's hair.

"An' Mom said that's why I have to go to bed when she's tired and I'm not, because

211

that's just the way life is. I was going to ask you why, Jeff, but I forgot and now I know. Even people have to do things just 'cause. Like trees and animals!"

"That's right, sport. Sometimes we may not be very happy about the things we have to do, but when we know it's necessary, we do it anyway. And now and then we may even do a cruel and unnecessary thing and leave it for someone else to clean up our mess."

"What's that mean, Jeff?" Yes, thought Eleanor, what does it mean?

"It means that I've got a big mess to clean up and I don't know how to go about doing it. Just like the long grass around the trunks of the trees, it will have to be cut out carefully, so as not to leave too many deep wounds and scars."

Phillip looked as bewildered as his mother felt. What was David saying? What was he trying to lead up to? "Don't you want to cut the grass, Jeff?"

"It will have to be done, son, but let's leave it for now and ask your mother if she feels like making us some lemonade."

Remembering what had recently been said, Phillip asked, "But she'll do it whether she feels like it or not, won't she Jeff? 'Cause that's what moms are for. For doing things for their kids, just like apple trees are for growing apples. Good thing my mom only has me to do things for."

They walked towards the house, David and Phillip a few paces behind Eleanor, and she heard her husband say, "But your mom hasn't always had just you to think about. She has been, over the years, a daughter, a wife, a mother and a woman. That's a lot for any one person to be, and it must have been hard sometimes to be all four together. It's no wonder your mom wants you to go to bed when she's tired."

"Yup," said Phillip. "Too bad she can't just stand around growing apples!"

Grant came back on Wednesday.

"Hello, Ellie," he said, sitting across from her in the arbour. "I'm sorry about the other night. I said a lot of things I shouldn't have, about your owing me . . . about Phillip. Will you forgive me?"

"Of course, Grant. I understand. You had a right to be upset. I shouldn't have sprung it on you like that. But this doesn't mean I've change . . ."

"Never mind that! I said a week. I want to wait until then! But there's no need to apologise for 'springing it on me'; there would have been no easy way to tell me he was your husband."

"Not 'was', Grant. Is."

"Yes. Well. Have you told the . . . told Phillip yet, who his 'friend' is?"

"No . . . no, I haven't. If . . . when I decide what I'm going to do . . . that'll be time enough to tell him. I will tell him, Grant, and I will let David have part of his time. I can't do anything else." She rose and left the arbour, having heard the school bus arrive.

Grant followed, and the puppy, frolicking at their heels, tripped him. "Why don't you keep that little pest on a leash?" he snapped, reverting to type.

"Why should I in my own yard?" she shot back.

"Because he'll have to get used to being on a leash when you move to the motel. I won't have him running loose there!"

Eleanor chose to ignore Grant's assumption that she would be moving to the motel. He had already said he wouldn't listen to a refusal before Friday, and that he wasn't going to take no for an answer, so what was the point in getting involved in an argument when Phillip was coming up the lane? "I thought you wouldn't have him . . . period?"

"We-ll . . . I've been thinking, it does seem a little unfair to the k . . . to Phillip."

So now he's willing to make the effort!

214

thought Eleanor with bitterness. Now that it's too late! But, said a small voice inside her, it was always too late. I wouldn't have married him anyway. If I had been going to, I wouldn't have put all those obstacles in the way.

At that moment the little boy dashed through the gate, swinging it closed quickly so the pup could not escape. He stooped, laughing, and deposited his lunch kit and plastic bag on the ground before scooping Casey up into his arms. The puppy wiggled in an ecstasy of joy and licked Phillip's face with a wet, pink tongue. "Cut it out Casey! Oh, that tickles! Hi, Mom! Where's Jeff?"

"Hi, dear. Have a nice day?" Phillip nodded while trying to keep his nose from being chewed off. "Aren't you going to say hello to Grant?" asked Eleanor, gently prodding her son's manners.

"Oh . . . yeah," without enthusiasm. "Hi, Grant. I didn't see your car."

"I rode over. Glider needed the exercise. Say, Phil, I hear you're a pretty good rider these days!" said Grant, attempting heartiness and achieving only falsity.

"Just on Siwash," replied Phillip sullenly, and Eleanor shot him a telling look.

"Oh," said Grant jovially, "if you can ride one horse, you can ride 'em all! Come on and give old Glider a try! He's in the field back of the barn."

Phillip shook his head, his mouth set in a rebellious line and started to walk away. Grant grabbed him by the shoulder. "I give a dollar bill to any kid that can stay on Glider for five minutes," he said coaxingly.

"No! No thank you," replied Phillip, remembering his manners for once.

"How about two dollars then . . . Five!"

"No! I don't want to ride on Glider!"

"Oh co . . ."

"Grant! Stop it!" shrieked Eleanor. "Don't try to bribe him!"

Grant let the child go and Phillip ran off in the direction of the woods, not even stopping at the house for his customary snack. The pup tumbled along with him, yelping.

"I . . . That was a mistake, wasn't it?" asked Grant miserably.

"Yes," grated Eleanor between her teeth, seething with fury. "It certainly was!"

"I'll go now . . . But I'll be back on Friday."

Oh! Would he never give up? "Don't bother!" Eleanor said to his departing back, but he either failed to hear her, or chose not to.

By Friday morning Eleanor was no nearer

knowing what her reply to Grant was going to mean in her future relationship with David. He had stayed completely away from her since Sunday when he cut the grass and made his cryptic comments, and she refused to allow herself to ask Phillip about him and his doings.

But one thing she did know was that the nearer her time of meeting with Grant grew, the more apprehensive she became. She did not fear that he would harm her physically, certainly not that! But she was still afraid . . . of something. If only David could be nearby, she thought, not in evidence, definitely not that, but near enough so she wouldn't feel so alone! Somehow, his presence in the cottage while she was refusing Grant would make her feel . . . stronger. Yes, that was it, stronger!

Eleanor walked slowly across the yard in front of her cottage, went up the path, and for the first time in seven years and ten months, stepped over the little trickling brook and into the daisy studded meadow, heading for the dark line of trees beyond. Where the path entered the forest, she stopped for a moment to look back.

The farmhouse stood as it always had, gaunt and grey, alone on top of its little hillock with the dark red barn off to one side. Faintly, through the branches of the spreading poplars, she could see the silver shingles of her own roof and the golden glint of sunlight shining on a window pane. She turned and went into the forest.

The path wound through the cool dimness, around tall trees and old, moss-covered nurse logs with delicate seedlings struggling for air and light. Huckleberry bushes dripped bright red berries from slender branches and long before she expected it, Eleanor found herself in the edge of the clearing.

It was raw and new, terrible looking as are most new clearings; the earth torn here and there, moss folded over in great pads exposing snake-like brown roots of the trees and underbrush. Sharp, jagged stumps stuck up like broken molars, but the ground had been smoothed and tidied all around the neat little log cabin which stood in the centre, its chimney rising askew against one side of the building. And there, just as she had been told, at the corner of the cabin, stood the dogwood tree, far bigger than it ought to have been.

Eleanor walked quietly nearer, feeling like an intruder. But how can I be? she asked. Isn't this my glade? Hadn't this been her special place until a brash young man had entered from out of the dark surrounds and claimed her for his own? Her heart thundered as she was struck by an overwhelming urge to see, just one more time, the little mossy hollow under the tree.

The stable was empty, neither David nor the horse were to be seen, and Eleanor stepped down into the cool, magic place of sweet memories.

It was shady as it had been before, and moss-filled, still, with feathery ferns hanging over the sides, creating the most secure and private of places. Eleanor stood in the centre of it for a moment, her eyes tightly shut, filling her mind with the memory of scent, of sound, and then she dropped to her knees in the thick mattress of moss. "Oh, David," she whispered. "I never forgot! How could you have for so many years?" A stray breeze whispered through the branches with a ghostly, derisive chuckle.

Eleanor ran from under the tree, and letting her feet follow the path which led to the forestry road, she soon came to the camper. Curiosity overcame her as she saw the door hanging open, and realised there was no one around, after all. If she wanted to talk to David, she might as well wait in comfort for his return.

She stepped inside the compact little home, noting the three-burner stove, the tiny fridge and oven, the neatly made bunk which jutted out over the cab of the truck. There was a window under that bunk which gave a view of the cab, and road beyond, and one more window on either side.

Through the window on her right, a beam of sun glanced in, picking up a reflection and flashing it in her eyes. Eleanor turned to see what was so bright, and was struck by the beauty of a gold filigree picture frame. She plucked it from its crooked perch above the stove, and stood staring for a long moment while all colour drained from her face.

With shaking hands she replaced the picture exactly as she had found it and stumbled from the camper, back into the woods, and ran home.

Grant was waiting for her, and Eleanor saw his car before he had seen her coming. She composed herself as best she could and walked sedately, her head held high, toward him.

"Well," he said heavily, "I'm ready . . . are you ready to agree to marry me?"

"No. I will not be able to marry you. I'm sorry, Grant." He could see there was no point in arguing just now. Something had given her a shock, and Grant was willing to bide his time some more if he had to.

"Are you going back to him?" he asked, somehow expecting the answer he got, but wishing that she had been able to say it with more expression in her voice, without that deathly look in her eyes.

"No, Grant. I'm going to sue David for divorce."

TEN

Grant stayed for an hour, but he could get Eleanor to commit herself no further than she had by her previous two statements. She would not marry him. She would not remain married to David. She did, however, agree to dine with Grant that night; a farewell dinner, she called it, and he agreed outwardly, while inwardly telling himself it was a celebration dinner, only she was still too upset to see it as such.

Phillip dragged 'Jeff' into the house with him that afternoon when school was finished. Eleanor heard them coming and steeled herself to meet David. "C'mon, Jeff! Let's ask her! I bet she's too tired to cook!" Then, catching sight of his mother, he said rapidly, "Mom! We got the fireplace ready to light today and the roof and floors and everything are finished and the glass is in the windows and we're going to cook hot dogs over the fire tonight for our supper. C'n I go Mom, and will you come too?"

Oh, no! she cried inside. Not tonight! Why tonight of all nights? How can I disappoint him with what I will have to tell him looming so close on the horizon? I'll have to go, and I'll have to keep up a good pretence of happiness for him! I can do it. I must do it! "Thank you, darling, I'd love to have you cook my dinner over the new fireplace. I did have other plans, but I'll go and use the phone in Bill's house and put them off until tomorrow. Would you like me to bring the popcorn and the long-handled popper, as my contribution?"

"Oh, Mom! Sure!" Phillip gave her a big hug, his skinny little arms digging into her waist, and over his head she saw David give her a grateful look. "Hurry! Hurry!" Phillip yelled, darting from her to the doorway. "I'm starving and we have to see if the chimney smokes before we can start cooking. Jeff went into town today and brought the wieners and buns."

"Tell you what, son," said David. "We'll go ahead and get the fire started and leave your mother to come as soon as she can. Then, if it smokes, she won't get it in her eyes."

"O.K.!" replied Phillip, and bounded off, the pup following close behind him.

"David . . . wait!" Eleanor spoke urgently as he made to go after Phillip. "I have to tell you . . . I . . . I'm sorry . . . I'm going to go into town on Monday and see a lawyer . . . to s-start divorce pro-proceedings . . .”

David's face turned a deathly shade of grey. He opened his mouth, but no words came. He closed his lids over almost black eyes for a moment and swallowed. Eleanor watched his reaction with growing horror. “The date,” he said in a strained voice, opening his eyes and looking at her, “the one you have to postpone . . . with Grant?”

She nodded, and said, “But not what . . .” It was useless to go on. David had bolted off into the late afternoon glare and for a long moment Eleanor watched his moving sil-houette as it became smaller and smaller until it finally disappeared into the trees.

Limply she called Grant, explained the situation, listened apathetically to his argu-ments, accepted his grudging agreement to put their date off until the following day, and called her baby sitter, to cancel.

Later, walking toward the woods with the setting sun making long, black shadows out across the meadow, Eleanor recalled the look on David's face when she had told him of her plans. Never had she seen a human being become so old, so ill, in such a short space of time! He had been grave before she spoke, but after her words had tumbled and tripped out, he had looked like death!

But why? Why should he have looked like that at the thought of losing her when he had that picture in his camper? She had been haunted by the memory of it all day! The beautiful woman, with her enormous dark eyes! The eyes so full of a deep, eternal sadness and wisdom! Long, curling black hair hung over her shoulder to mingle with the equally dark hair of the lovely little girl in her arms. The child was the image of her mother, with eyes just as dark, but gleaming with a life, a joy in life, that was lacking in those of the woman. Why, when he had that portrait signed 'With deepest love from Manuela and Juanita', had he come back to her, to plain, ordinary Eleanor whom he had chosen to forget for all those years?

Could it be that the woman had somehow found out about her, Eleanor, and sent David away? Or had they died, the beautiful Manuela and the child? And at their death, and only then, had David remembered another wife, another child, and come back to try again?

As Eleanor's feet beat an unerring path to David, her heart, her mind, were doing the same, for he was part of her, even while she could not accept that which he had done. He had been right not to take the risk of telling her the reason for his long absence. Knowing how she felt about the years she had spent alone, he must have known, too, that the knowledge that he had spent them in another woman's arms, another woman's home, would destroy her faith in herself. It had. Where did I go wrong? she asked herself. Where did I fail him? Was I too young? Was it the fact that I was too ill with Phillip to go to him? Was it that he knew how I hated having to leave my father? What?

As the confused thoughts whipped back and forth through her mind, Eleanor had been walking steadily along the forest path, and found herself once more in the clearing. Phillip was waiting impatiently in the door of the cabin.

"Mom! Mom! Hurry up!" he called excitedly. "The chimney draws like it should and Jeff says that's 'cause it's crooked. I made it crooked, Mom, 'cause I was too short to reach up and get all the rocks in just right. Oh, good, you 'membered the popcorn! Look at that horse-shoe!" He dragged her into the doorway and pointed up at the lintel, where on a big nail, hung a horse-shoe. "It's mine, Mom! My very own! Jeff and Si gave it to me for my birthday!" He paused for breath, and then went on, "Did you know that me 'n' Jeff're going to live here in the summers for as many summers as I like? Oh, I forgot, Jeff says we have to ask you first, Mom. Can I? Huh, Mom? Can I?" His trusting eyes searched hers for the answer, and then he added, "I'll be close to home, Mom, and I'll come and visit you every day!"

"I don't see why not, son," she said with what she hoped was a smile. "If you want to, you certainly may!"

David appeared in the doorway of a small room at one end of the cabin. He approached the other two with a travesty of a smile on his face. "I see you made it," he observed unnecessarily, relieving her of the popcorn and popper. His eyes were bleak and dark. "I'm glad . . . for Phillip's sake." One hand touched her elbow, lightly, but burning, nevertheless. "Come in, Eleanor."

The interior of the cabin was lit by the glow of the fire and the small amount of daylight admitted by the two tiny windows. Against one wall stood a hand-made table, its top of pine boards, its legs of solid timbers, planed and sanded to a smooth finish. There were three chairs made of poles with braided cedar bark woven into seats, and three bowls made from maple burls lay on the table, polished to a high shine which caught the firelight and threw it softly against the wall.

The dim doorway from which David had emerged showed the end of a large, built-in bunk and Eleanor let her eyes flick past that and come to rest on the fireplace which was a smaller replica of the one in her cottage.

"Pretty good, huh, Mom?" asked Phillip with loud excitement. "See my bunk?" And he ran to the narrow, deep bunk which was against the wall right next to the fireplace. "This is where I'll sleep on those cold winter nights when the wind screams down from the Yukon and the wolves howl around outside looking for a way in. But they won't get me because I'll be warm and snug in my bed by the fire and Jeff'll be warm and snug in his bed with his sweet lady and when the fire burns low it'll be my job to throw more wood on it!" He sucked in a great gulp of air and would surely have gone on breaking his mother's heart had 'Jeff' not intervened.

"Phil," he said, and his quiet voice yet seemed to fill the empty corners of the cabin. "That was only a game of pretend that we played. Why not show your mother the spit where we're going to cook the bear steaks and moose roasts and hot dogs?"

After the hot dogs in lieu of moose roast had been devoured, Phillip squatted in front of the fire, his face glowing red as he vigorously shook the corn popper and listened enthralled to the clatter of kernels bursting against the lid.

Steam rose from the small pan of butter melting near the coals and when the sound of popping had ceased, Phillip turned to David, his face the epitome of joy. "Think it's done?" he asked, and at David's nod, carefully carried the popper to the table where David poured it into the three bowls.

Eleanor picked up the pan of butter and stood holding it while Phillip placed the bowls, one by one, in front of each chair. "One for papa bear, one for mama bear and one for boy bear."

His mother blinked away the tears which suddenly burned in her eyes but not before her sharp-eyed little son had noticed. "What's the matter, Mom?"

She smiled at him. "Just a little smoke from the fire."

"Aw, Mom . . . I bet you was going to cry 'cause I said boy bear, not baby bear. What we need is a baby so you won't mind being a boy."

Eleanor couldn't prevent her glance flying to David's. The knowledge that there was that possibility was in both of them, although until this moment of tacit communication, neither had admitted even to themselves, that it was there. "I don't mind having a boy, not a baby," said Eleanor hurriedly, her voice sounding unnaturally high. "What I think we need right now is Goldilocks! My popcorn porridge is too hot!"

Over Phillip's giggles, David spoke quietly in Eleanor's ear. "I'm sure that could be arranged. Shall I try the motel?"

The bitterness in his tone was too much for Eleanor. She wheeled and ran out the cabin door, tears streaming down her face, sobs choking her as she headed for home. David caught her at the edge of the clearing.

"Eleanor! I'm sorry, I'm sorry! Come back! Let's not ruin his housewarming party for him!"

She buried her face in her hands, trying to regain control. She trembled violently as he held her shoulders, pulling her back against his chest. At last she raised her head. "I'm all right," she said dully. "I'm ready to go back now."

They sat in the firelight in the warm little cabin, on the rough, hard boards of the floor and sang silly songs for an hour, accompanied by Eleanor on the guitar which David had produced. When Phillip was yawning too much to continue singing, Eleanor put the guitar up on the table and said, "Come on, son. Time to go home and get you to bed."

"Can I sleep here, Mom? It's warm enough."

David looked directly at Eleanor for the first time since he had brought her back. His slate-grey eyes begged.

"How about tomorrow night, Phil?" she suggested. "I have to go out and Cindy can't come. I had her booked for tonight, but I cancelled and tomorrow she's sitting for the Peters." Eleanor turned to David to explain, "Cindy Exley's my regular baby sitter . . . so if you wouldn't mind . . . ?"

His words, calm and quiet, belied the expression on his face. "I don't mind, Eleanor. I'll walk you home."

Eleanor tried to be good company for Grant. He ordered champagne and raised his glass in a toast. "To your freedom," he said. She tried to laugh at his jokes, with an effort made her arms and legs go through the motions of dancing. She made a brave attempt to put some animation into her voice, but she knew it was all for nothing. "I'll take you home," said Grant. "I don't think you're really with me tonight."

At the door to the cottage, when she

turned to say 'thank you' to him, and he lifted her face to kiss her, Eleanor turned aside and his lips met her ear. "Good bye, Grant. I'm sorry."

"Good bye? Oh, no. Not that easily, Eleanor. Good night, maybe, but I am going to go with you on Monday . . . just to be sure that you really go!"

"I'll go, Grant. But it doesn't mean a change where my feelings for you are concerned. I'm sorry!" she repeated, and slipped inside, closing the door on him.

Eleanor, planning to sleep late on Sunday to make the day seem as short as possible, was surprised to look at her clock and see that it read only half-past six when Phillip's cold little hands touched her.

"Mom," he said plaintively. "Mom, wake up! Jeff's sick. He got up a little while ago and went to the camper for some medicine and when he didn't come back I went to look for him and he's lying on the floor. He won't sit up or talk or nothing! Will you come?"

Before Phillip had finished talking Eleanor was dragging on a pair of jeans, ripping her nightgown off and putting a tee-shirt over her head. On her way through the door, she said, "Did you touch him? Is he hot?"

"The door was shut and I couldn't open it so I climbed up and looked in the window and he's lying there all funny looking. I banged on the side window and called him but he didn't move."

Eleanor dragged her son by the hand as they pelted across the creek, up the meadow and into the woods. By the time they reached the camper she had a terrible stitch in her side, her head was swimming, and her breath coming in laboured gasps. She wrenched open the door and knelt beside David. A sob escaped her when she saw he was breathing. But he was lying too still! And he was hot!

Frantically she tried to recall the incubation time for measles; if her estimate were right, this was about the day he should be getting them, if he were going to. And it looked very much as if he were!

"Wake up, David," she said, shaking him gently by the shoulder. "Darling, come on! I have to get you home to bed!" But he failed to respond, just lay there, breathing stertorously.

Eleanor turned to her son who was standing just outside the door of the camper, his eyes wide and frightened. He still panted from his frantic run. "Phillip," she asked, "where does Jeff keep the keys to the truck?" She conquered the tendency her voice had to quiver, telling herself, I must keep calm, I must keep calm!

"In his pants pocket, Mom," was the logical reply, and she dug down into his pockets until she found the key ring. "Darling," she said to Phillip, "I want you to come in here and sit on the floor so you can hold Jeff's head in your lap. I'm going to drive the truck home and the road is rough. I don't want him to bump his head. That's the way . . . just like that. Put both arms under his chin, but don't choke him. I'm going to close the door, and I'll see you in a few minutes."

With trembling hands Eleanor checked out the gears of the truck and started the engine. She let the clutch out too quickly and it jerked violently, stalling. Slowly, Eleanor, she told herself, slow and steady . . .

Gently, inch by painful inch, she set the truck in motion, drove carefully along the forestry track and once on the highway, speeded up to well in excess of the limit. At this hour on a Sunday morning, there was no traffic, and she made good time, turning into the driveway of the farm less than fifteen minutes after Phillip had wakened her.

There was no driveway leading to the cottage, so Eleanor put the truck in bull-low and drove it down the steep, grassy slope, pulling up just by the rose arbour. She swung the back door open and found Phillip exactly as she had left him, David's head cradled on his lap, his eyes still wide with fright. "All right, son?"

"He's talkin' funny, Mom!"

Eleanor held David's head gently while her son slithered out from under. "That's nothing to worry about, son," she said evenly. "He has a fever like I had, and I got better, didn't I?" A reassured Phillip would be a more helpful Phillip, and a busy Phillip would be a boon to her!

"I want you to get me the wheelbarrow, and bring it just as quickly as you can. Run!" Phillip ran.

When he returned, the wheelbarrow bumping along in front of him, Eleanor smiled at him, hoping her mouth looked more cheerful than it felt. "Good boy! Now go get that long board out of the orchard and lean it up the front steps and open the door."

While Phillip was doing what she asked, Eleanor was busy herself. She dragged the inert weight of her husband to the door of the camper and rolled him as gently as she could into the barrow. Phillip, who had just opened the front door, stood staring in amazement as his mother trundled the laden barrow across the lawn, up the board and right inside, leaving a muddy streak from the wheel on the carpet as she disappeared into her bedroom. He followed right behind her and was in time to see her lift the handles of the wheelbarrow high enough to roll his friend Jeff unceremoniously onto the bed.

"Phillip," Eleanor said quietly, "take the key to the big house and go up and call the operator. Tell her where you live, and that your mom needs help with a man who might have the measles. Say he has a high temperature."

Phillip nodded uncertainly, and she said, "Can you remember all that? Tell me what you're going to tell the operator."

"My mom needs help for Jeff 'cause he's got a bad fever and maybe measles and I live at Barnes Dairy on the ninety-six."

"That's right. And ask her to send a doctor. It doesn't matter which one. Off you go and come right back!"

While her son was away Eleanor wrestled David's clothing off him and tumbled him into the sheets she herself had so recently left. He tossed and turned, moaned now and then, and began shaking as if his bones were attached to a paint mixer. She held him when he tried to get up, at one point sitting on him and gritting her teeth as his fingers bit into her arm. All the while she talked, trying to get through to him.

"Darling, darling, don't. Lie still, David. I love you and I want to help you! You must stay in the bed! No! You can't go until the doctor comes!"

His eyes were wide open and staring wildly at her, but she knew it was not her he was seeing. Whatever he was looking at in his nightmare world was a terrible, incredibly wicked thing who was trying to prevent him from doing what he wanted to do. "Go away . . . go away . . . Let me be! I want to die! There's no need for you to torture me by keeping me alive when they are both dead! Let me go . . . let me go to her . . . I need her . . ." And his head lolled loosely on the pillow as David fell horrifyingly quiet.

"What was he sayin' Mom?" Phillip was back, and by the look of fright on his face, had seen the contorted face, heard the tortured words.

"It's all right, Phillip. He's just having a nightmare like you used to have, remember. Is the doctor coming?"

"Yes. The operator let me talk to Dr. Grimes my own-self," he said, not without pride. "I told him that Jeff was sick and would he please come and help you make him better 'cause he has measles and is real hot. He asked me if Jeff was big like me or little, and I told him Jeff was big like a daddy and he said he'd be here in a flash. If Jeff's havin' nightmares whyn't you rock him like you did me? It made my bad dreams go away."

"Yes, dear. I will. You go and feed Casey and make yourself some toast or something. And don't forget that Siwash will need some breakfast, too."

By the time the doctor arrived, David was shaking again, and muttering. Eleanor did rock him as she had told Phillip she would; she held him close and when the doctor hammered on the door, David's clinging hands nearly prevented her leaving.

After an examination and much head-scratching, Dr. Grimes looked up at Eleanor who was standing at the foot of the bed, tense and worried. "Where the heck's this man been living?"

"P-Peru . . . as far as I know."

The doctor smiled with what might have been relief. "O.K., then. That's the answer. I was wondering how I was going to explain a case of malaria in a remote corner of the interior of B.C.!"

"Malaria?"

Dr. Grimes nodded, looking pleased with himself. "I'm pretty sure that's what it is, but the lab will have to confirm it. In the meantime a dose of Atabrine wouldn't go amiss. I'll give him a shot of a different anti-pyretic for now and drop by later with the Atibrine. Can you manage to look after him here? The hospital's crowded. It won't be much, or for long, but he'll feel pretty bad for a couple or three days."

After Eleanor had assured the doctor that she had every intention of caring for the sick man herself, he gave her a few brief instructions and left.

For the rest of the day Eleanor divided her time between caring for David and trying to keep Phillip calm. He paced and worried, fretted and asked a million questions, one of which she had been expecting for hours. Yet when the question came, she felt her heart flip and her mouth dry. What if David was about to change his mind again? What if the woman and child in the picture, the ones he was raving about so much, were not to be forgotten after all? But still . . .

"Mom, how come you keep calling Jeff 'David', and 'darling'?"

"Because," she said slowly, after a pause, "his name really is David. I called him darling because I love him."

"Well, if you love Jeff, how come you're going to marry Grant?"

"I'm not going to marry Grant."

"Then are you going to marry Jeff?"

"Phillip . . . I'm . . . I'm already married to Je . . . to David. He's your father, Phil."

"You mean the one what went away before I got borned and got lost and never came back? That one?"

"That's the one," she nodded.

"Well, how come he didn't come back?" asked Phillip indignantly.

"I don't know, Phillip."

"Well, I guess it doesn't matter, does it Mom? I mean he is my dad, and I love him and he did come back, so I guess we just got to keep him, huh, Mom?"

Eleanor swallowed hard. The acceptance of a child! The forgiveness! How much time she'd wasted by not having the same qualities herself! "I guess we just got to keep him, Phil," she whispered.

"Hey, Mom, how come you're cryin'?"

Monday morning dawned and Eleanor agreed with her son that he should stay home from school just that once, so that he could help her if she needed it. He helped her all right, and she could have rung his neck, or kissed him . . . or something!

David was having a quiet spell so Eleanor had slipped into the kitchen for something to eat, when she heard Phillip yelling loudly, triumphantly . . .

"Hey Grant! Didja know that Jeff is David my dad and he came back and he's got malaria and we're going to keep him 'cause he is our dad even if he did go away for a long time!"

She got to the kitchen door in time to see Grant roughly push Phillip out of his path, to see him step on Casey's paw and stride determinedly toward her. The expression on her face was enough to tell him that Phillip had spoken the truth.

"Ellie . . . oh, Ellie. I never gave up hope until this moment . . ."

"I'm sorry Grant. I told you to and . . . I'm sorry."

Grant walked back up the hill to his car, seeing nothing, not even the rather nasty little boy who stood, holding his puppy, caressing the sore paw, staring after the man, and sticking out an impudent little tongue at the departing back.

David came to during the night. It was very dark, not even a glimmer of moonlight lit the windows of the camper, and he wondered why this bunk was so soft and warm and what was causing that lovely scent which tickled his nostrils. Slowly it dawned on him that he was not in the camper, he was in Eleanor's bed. It must be a dream, he thought, but her warmth by his side, her steady, even breathing told him it was true. He reached out a tentative hand and ran a finger-tip down her spine. She murmured and turned into his arms, nestling close.

He put his lips to her hair, afraid to move, afraid to wake her and send her flying from his arms again. For these few moments in time he would pretend that this was how it would always be.

The rhythm of her breathing changed and he felt her arms tighten around him and heard her whisper in the dark and quiet night, "David? You awake?"

"I'm awake Eleanor. Was it malaria?"

"Yes, David," very quietly.

"What day is it?"

"Probably early Tuesday morning."

"What happened Monday?"

"Nothing much. The same as Sunday; chills, fever. The doctor came twice Sunday, once Monday. You're something of an irregular experience for him."

"Did you go . . . to town?"

"No, David."

"Are you going to?"

"Not unless you want me to."

She felt a tremor run through him. "I want you to stay here, Eleanor. Forever."

"That's what I want too David if you want me," she said in a rushed, frightened voice.

"I want you. I love you, sweet lady . . ." He was unable to go on for a moment. "I love you more than life, Eleanor. More than anyone."

"Man . . . Manuela?" she whispered, choking on the word, but knowing it must be said. "Manuela and Juanita?"

"God! I must have been doing some raving!" David sounded astonished, bewildered.

"A little. But I saw the picture in the truck, David . . . on Friday when I was going to ask you to be near when I told Grant I wouldn't marry him. I went looking for you and I found them . . . They are both very beautiful, David . . . or maybe I should say 'were'. Maybe someday when I can face it you will tell me about them, about what happened to them . . . you talked when you were sick . . . said, 'My wife is dead. I want to die too.' I was horribly jealous, David, and for a time I hated you, but when you wanted to die I couldn't let you. I love you and I'm just grateful that you came back to me when you lost her."

David was silent for a long time.

Eleanor thought he must have fallen asleep once more, when he spoke in a husky voice. "And you still want me, Eleanor?"

"I always have. Like I told you, on Friday, I hated you and them, even the little girl. I resented the fact that you had been with them while I was all alone, nursing my own child through all the childhood ailments, trying to raise him without your moral support. But you loved them and I can understand that and when you said they were dead, I couldn't hate them or you any longer. You are my husband, Phillip's father. I told him, too." She raised her head and kissed his mouth tenderly, knowing he was too weak to kiss her. "I only hope Phillip will make up in some ways for your loss of the little girl."

"Oh, Eleanor, Eleanor, my own sweet lady! God! How can I tell you?" He held her to him, rocking her as if in pain, his hands slipped into her hair and he kissed her, showing he was not as weak as she had thought.

"Tell me what?" she asked.

"Sweetheart, if one of us has to get sick before I'm allowed into your bed, I'm going to take up walking in the coldest rain I can find and I'll drag you along with me!"

It was Saturday. David, Eleanor and Phillip were having breakfast when Bill walked in. He stared around in amazement at what appeared to be a happy, family meal in progress. "Say, didn't you have a beard the last time I saw you?"

David nodded, rubbed a hand over his still faintly yellow jaw and reached out to shake hands.

"Bill, I passed!" said Phillip proudly. "I'll be in Grade Two in September!"

"Good for you!" Bill smiled at the little boy, but Eleanor could see him giving David an odd little glance out of the corner of his eye.

"Bill," she said, pouring him a cup of coffee, "this man's an imposter. He told you his name was Jeff Davidson, didn't he?"

Bill nodded, mystified, and not a little concerned for Eleanor. "I'd like you to be the first of my friends to meet David Jefferson, my husband."

Bill's jaw dropped. "You're kidding! Why didn't you tell me that before? Where you been, man?"

David grinned. He had already told this to Eleanor and Phillip, but he recited it for Bill's benefit, anyway. "Peru, Chile, Brazil, Peru again, Venezuela, Peru, and Colombia. I left Bogota when the medics there told me if I didn't get out of the tropics I'd become a basket case. I wasn't sure about still having a place to return to here, but it seems I did."

"Seems so," said Bill, stirring sugar into his coffee. He gave Eleanor a look, stirred some more, and glowered. She touched his hand and smiled at him. Her eyes, her face, the new glow about her cried out, "Be nice to him Bill! It's my life, my business and don't spoil it by disliking him for my sake!" He slowly smiled back at her, and Eleanor knew he would accept David.

"Tell him about going to jail!" cried Phillip to his father. That was by far his favourite of all the stories that David had told.

"Jail?"

"Well, my son," and the smile on David's face as he looked at the child removed all last traces of doubt from Bill's mind. This was right! ". . . my son," repeated David, "is quite impressed by the fact that I once spent three weeks in a hot, foul little stone cell for having stolen a fish from a street vendor. I hadn't, but I stayed there until the idiot finally admitted to having turned his back long enough for a cat to take it. He wanted the money it was worth, and chose me to accuse. I was in a stubborn mood, refused to pay up, and of course I didn't have the fish on me, but laws are funny here and there. That's all there was to it, but Phil thinks it's great."

"Stupid things people will do for a principle," said Bill. Then, "Look, Ellie, what I came down for is to get your permission to renovate your dad's office and make a nursery out of it. It's the only room on the ground floor that's big enough, that we aren't using already."

"I don't really think my permission will be required, Bill. You see, we were thinking of selling the farm . . . to you and Kathy. If you want it."

"If! Ellie, you know we do! But what about Phil? I thought you always wanted to keep it in case he wanted it one day?"

"He won't." That was David. "He'll have the Anderson place if he wants that. I bought it."

"Wow! You two'll have to get a move on if you want to fill up that old barn of a house! I need your dad's place Ellie, for my three to grow up in, but that place! It's a mansion!"

"We'll fill it!" said David and Eleanor in unison, and when the laughter died down, she said, "When do the babies get released, and when's Kathy coming home from her mother's?"

"She's home. The babies come home next week. That's why we want to get a nursery arranged."

"She's home? And we're sitting here? Let's go! I'm dying to see her!" Eleanor grabbed David's hand. "Come on, darling. But be prepared for a bit of ice, won't you?" she added for his ears alone.

"I am," he replied quietly. "I can take it as long as I have you. I saw Bill's reaction."

Kathy was distinctly cool until Bill took her aside. "Look at Ellie," he said severely. "The sun rose inside her this morning! Now be nice to her husband!"

A laughing group comprised of four adults, one small boy and a puppy set to with a will to convert a dingy old office into a bright shiny nursery big enough for three of everything.

As the two men shoved the heavy, dark old furniture into the hallway, the women went along behind with brooms, mops and dusters. The one small boy and the puppy got in the way.

"Hey, Je . . . Dad, what's this?" asked Phillip, pulling a yellowish piece of paper out of a crack in the back of the desk which had once been his grandfather's. David didn't even look. Father-like, he said, "Ask your mother."

Eleanor took the paper from her son, opened it and said, "Why, it's to me. I must have missed it when I cleared out the desk." She began to read aloud.

'My dear little Ellie.
I am going to die and I know you will find this when it's too late for your hatred to hurt me if it turns out I was wrong to take the chance I did. When I saw that you had stopped grieving for your man, I . . .'

At that point David lunged at her, trying to snatch the paper from her hand. "No!" he cried hoarsely, "No, darling! Don't read that!"

She spun out of his reach, her face white, her eyes large and dark, and continued reading hurriedly.

'. . . wrote to the forestry department official who had sent the wire saying he was missing. I told him that you and the boy had both died the day he was born. If your man was ever found, then this is why he never came back. I did this because I could see you had got over him and he would have taken you away. I told him I would fight, girl, and I did. What I did was wrong, even though I'm sure he will never read the letter. I want you to try to forgive your old,

Dad.'

Eleanor let the paper fall to the floor, and turned to walk slowly out of the house, as if sleeping. David went after her, and when Phillip would have followed, Kathy held him back, saying, "No, dear. Let your parents have a few minutes alone."

Eleanor knelt beside her bed, her face buried in the covers, her mind a total blank. David stood beside her, his hand on her hair, not speaking, but when her shoulders began heaving and deep sobs tore from her he picked her up and held her, sitting in the big chair, letting the storm of weeping run its course.

"He stole seven years from us!"

"You see why I couldn't tell you?"

"I see why you thought you couldn't. But you must have hated him too when you found out we were alive, as much as I hate him at this moment. Or did you think I was part of the deception, too?"

"For a very short time, yes. Until Phillip told me that Grant said you were in love with a ghost. Then I knew it had been him, and him alone. I don't hate him anymore, darling and I don't want you to, either. He said he'd fight."

"He said he'd win, too. He almost did, David! He almost did!"

"Almost isn't close enough; he didn't win and if I had remembered his saying that, if I had taken it seriously, I would have checked. I should have! I'll never forgive myself for not doing it!"

"No . . . you had a letter from him . . . I had no proof, no reason to believe that you were dead. I should have kept on making enquiries, especially after he died. But I'm glad about one thing, David; you weren't as lonely as I was all those years. I'm glad that, even loving what you thought was just my memory, you found some happiness. Can you tell me what happened to them . . . to Manuela and Juanita?"

"Remember I told you about Juan Mercado, the man who survived the fall down the cliff, then died in the rapids? That he, too had a pregnant wife? That was . . . is Manuela. The child is Juanita . . . his child, Eleanor, not mine. His wife, not mine . . . never mine. When I got out I went to see her. They were very poor, darling and I had no one. I became Juanita's godfather and helped them financially until Manuela remarried. I kept the picture because I do love my little goddaughter and I am fond of her mother. I never loved her, Eleanor! How could I, when there was you?"

"Yet you would have let me go on believing you had loved her, at least lived with her, rather than tell me what Dad had done?"

"You had forgiven me for what you thought was my infidelity, so I didn't have to tell you anything else. I would rather have had you thinking that than have you as you are now, hating the memory of your father. I know how much the two of you meant to each other and I wanted to spare you that."

"Would you have told me . . . to keep me from marrying Grant?"

"I wouldn't have had to. I knew you would never marry him."

"Then why did you look so terrible when I told you I was getting a divorce?"

"Because I knew I would have to tell you about your father, and I didn't know if you'd believe me without proof. I destroyed the letter. Who wants something like that lying around?"

"I would have believed you, David," she said, looking up into his eyes, her own full of love. "I will always believe you."

For a long time there was silence in the

little cottage until the shuffling of small, sneakered feet in the doorway could have been heard by the two in the chair, had they been listening. They were not, but they did hear an over-loud, piping voice saying with disgust, "Aw, come on, Casey! Let's go play! All those guys want to do is kiss!"

The employees of Thorndike Press hope you have enjoyed this Large Print book. All our Thorndike and Wheeler Large Print titles are designed for easy reading, and all our books are made to last. Other Thorndike Press Large Print books are available at your library, through selected bookstores, or directly from us.

For information about titles, please call:

(800) 223-1244

or visit our Web site at:

www.gale.com/thorndike
www.gale.com/wheeler

To share your comments, please write:

Publisher
Thorndike Press
295 Kennedy Memorial Drive
Waterville, ME   04901